Wyatt Bent To Kiss Tallulah In The Moonlight,

wondering, Who was this woman who cared so much for others, who tended the old and the sick and the worried with her heart? Who protected his daughter as fiercely as if his child was her own flesh and blood? Who didn't think of herself as a desirable woman?

She was desirable, all right. And Wyatt could think of one man who wanted her—right here and now.

Dear Reader:

Welcome to Silhouette Desire - provocative, compelling, contemporary love stories written by and for today's woman. These are stories to treasure.

Each and every Silhouette Desire is a wonderful romance in which the emotional and the sensual go hand in hand. When you open a Desire, you enter a whole new world - a world that has, naturally, a perfect hero just waiting to whisk you away! A Silhouette Desire can be light-hearted or serious, but it will always be satisfying.

We hope you enjoy this Desire today - and will go on to enjoy many more.

Please write to us:

Jane Nicholls
Silhouette Books
PO Box 236
Thornton Road
Croydon
Surrey
CR9 3RU

Mr Easy
CAIT LONDON

SILHOUETTE
Desire

*First published in Great Britain in 1995
by Silhouette Books, Eton House, 18-24 Paradise Road,
Richmond, Surrey TW9 1SR*

© Lois Kleinsasser 1995

*Silhouette, Silhouette Desire and Colophon are
Trade Marks of Harlequin Enterprises II B.V.*

ISBN 0 373 05919 1

22-9509

Made and printed in Great Britain

CAIT LONDON

lives in the Missouri Ozarks, but loves to travel the northwest's gold-rush and cattle-drive trails every summer. She loves research trips, meeting people and going to Native American dances. Ms London is an avid reader who loves to paint, play with computers and grow herbs (particularly scented geraniums right now). She is a national bestselling author who has received awards for her novels. She also writes historical romances under another pseudonym.

Three is Cait's lucky number; she has three daughters, and the events in her life have always been in threes. "I love writing for Silhouette," she says. "One of the best perks about all this hard work is the thrilling reader response and the warm, snug sense that I have given readers an enjoyable, entertaining gift."

Other Silhouette Books by Cait London

Silhouette Desire

The Loving Season
Angel vs. MacLean
The Pendragon Virus
The Daddy Candidate
Midnight Rider
The Cowboy
Maybe No, Maybe Yes
The Seduction of Jake Tallman
Fusion
The Bride Says No

To my good friends, Ben and Pauline.
I love you.

One

Fly fishing and women required patience, Wyatt decided as he expertly tied waxed red thread around the trout hook. The third Saturday in May—the opening of trout season in Montana—was the perfect time to try his new design. The lure would tempt the browns and rainbow trout hovering in the stream near the cabin. Trout preferred lures that resembled the stream's hatching insects.

Edgy, emotional, fiercely protective women like Tallulah Jane Ames needed just as distinctive bait.

Wyatt wanted a showdown; he had chosen to take his stand in the remote cabin near the rippling, trout-infested stream. The Montana stream provided a variety of conditions to test his world-famous lures, and the privacy for his showdown with Tallulah. A quiet loner, Wyatt wanted to study his opponent, noting her weaknesses before offering her his bait.

Wyatt's usual opponents were sleek and iridescent, gliding through streams and rivers; Tallulah's five-foot-eleven-inch height was topped by smooth, reddish gold hair. Parted on the side, its silky length curled when it reached her shoulders. Whenever she sighted Wyatt, her eyes turned smoke gray behind her big glasses, which were usually delicately spotted with her restaurant's daily special.

Tallulah had made herself the guardian angel of the two people Wyatt wanted to know better—his daughter, Fallon, and his granddaughter, Miracle. Fallon's last name was Smith now, changed long ago by her mother, who didn't want her found. Taken from him as a baby, Fallon didn't even know her father's name was Remington.

When he'd first stepped into Tallulah's café, the Tall Order, three months ago, she had glanced at him. Then she had given Danny Rollins, who sat beside Wyatt at the counter, a big smile and another piece of pie.

When Wyatt saw Fallon, a part of him lit with happiness, even as his heart tightened with sadness because she did not know him. She had been ripped away from him too soon.

When he had turned back to Tallulah, she had sloshed a glass of water onto the counter. A quick slap of a menu and a dark, hostile scowl followed. Tight anger laced through her "What do you want?" and her curls had caught the bright February light, shimmering to the beat of Elvis Presley's "All Shook Up."

For three months, Tallulah had blocked his path to his daughter. Since Fallon worked as a waitress for Tallulah and resided under her caring wing, Wyatt had little opportunity to introduce himself in the gentle way he had planned.

He was going to take Tallulah out of his life stream...he'd study her, find her weakness and set the hook.

Wyatt carefully snipped the fly's bristly wings with the scissors that he had designed especially for the task and that bore his company's trademark.

Tallulah had a way of letting everyone know exactly what and who pleased her. Since she had grown up in the tiny

Montana town of Elegance and loved everyone in it, they received "seconds-on-the-house" slices of Tallulah's famed pies. "Everyone" included a swarm of ex-boyfriends, passing truckers and anyone but Wyatt. Tallulah's immediate distrust and dislike of him unexpectedly riffled his usually calm emotional waters.

Wyatt resented her interference with his daughter and he resented not being offered a second slice of pie. He studied the fly he was creating with the patience, training and logic that had made him an expert fisherman and lure designer.

When he encountered Tallulah Jane, "Stretch," in her element—the café and surrounded by her lifelong friends, and occasionally bopping with a horde of ex-boyfriends to the fifties songs playing from her jukebox—Wyatt's famed logic slid to another galaxy.

Wyatt's fingers tightened momentarily on the feathered and chenille-wrapped shank of the hook. Before releasing the lure, he allowed himself a frown, a rare display of emotion.

He wanted that damned second slice of pie, offered by the one-and-only Tallulah.

The juicy pastry had become as elusive and prized as a bandit trophy trout.

If he could successfully psych out every species of trout in the United States, England and other countries, he could find out what made one woman tick. Then he'd get to her....

At his age, forty-four, the whole matter of baiting a trap for a reluctant woman, enticing her into his lair and hooking her on his line seemed a little weird.

Fantasizing about being offered a second piece of Tallulah's delicious pies was ridiculous for a man as streetwise, methodical and determined as he was ... a man who moved without entanglements, keeping alert for any word of his daughter and willing to relocate to the town she now called home. The last magic and fantasy he'd experienced was the birth of Fallon, twenty-one years ago.

Wyatt and his daughter had lost a lifetime. Though he had kept a close check on Fallon through his attorney, Wyatt realized that he couldn't introduce himself to her too soon. For two years, he'd wrapped up business commitments and had prayed that she wouldn't move. He also knew that Fallon needed time to feel safe, to nestle in the bosom of the small warm town before he entered her life. For her sake, Wyatt pushed down his eagerness to know his daughter; she'd had a lifetime share of upheavals.

Once Tallulah took the bait, once he routed out her weaknesses, he would remove her from the game. A man who kept his heart closed to others, Wyatt did not consider telling Tallulah anything about his relationship to Fallon and Miracle. An open book, easily read by the community, Tallulah could cause problems and complicate an already difficult matter.

He'd never been a perverse man. However, now he admitted that somewhere in the murky depths of his scarred heart leaped a certain joy when he thought of Tallulah coming to him—like a reluctant trout drawn by his carefully crafted lure.

If Fallon and Miracle weren't involved, Wyatt would almost enjoy reeling Tallulah in.

Leroy's pink-and-black snout bumped gently at the worn denim covering Wyatt's thigh and he reached to rub the pig's bristly forehead. He allowed himself to be comforted by Leroy's nuzzling. *With a pig, you always know where you stand,* Wyatt thought darkly. He tried to remember what could have started the silent fury in Tallulah that had arisen the first moment she'd seen him and erupted every time he walked into her café.

The nuzzling at his thigh reminded him of Leroy's presence. Because an eighty-pound, potbellied, black-and-pink pig clashed with the image of Tallulah, who was long and lean, Wyatt flipped a raisin into the air, then pointed to Leroy's pallet. Wyatt didn't want distractions while he thought of Tallulah.

Leroy, who resented the remote Montana cabin's lack of a television set, caught the raisin neatly. His potbelly swayed as he stalked to his pallet, where he lay down, mourning his favorite television show—the provocative "Miss Swine"—and glaring at Wyatt with beady eyes. Leroy preferred his comfortable bed in the small pull-along camper trailer, which Wyatt had parked just outside Elegance; the porker also resented the frequent fishing trips to the cabin.

Wyatt returned to perfecting his latest pricey design for trout fly fishing, the Sniggler. His fingers moved deftly, fashioning beaver hair and chenille around the tiny hook gripped in the vise.

Wyatt flicked his finger over the lure, testing the hackle, the small tuft of hair that resembled a hatching insect's wings. The early-afternoon sun lit the reddish tinge on the beaver hair, reminding Wyatt of Tallulah's bright, silky mane.

He studied the bristly little affair concealing a trout hook and jotted another design note for his partner, who handled the manufacturing and distribution of W.R.'s expensive lures.

Because Tallulah was a fighter just like the trout his lures enticed, Wyatt expected a battle before she took his carefully crafted bait. An expert at playing a fighting fish, Wyatt realized that showdown time with Tallulah loomed before him. He mentally flipped the picture of a beautiful, elusive, wary trout, a silvery arc rising high over a rippling stream, fighting the line, to the picture of Tallulah—

The picture didn't fit.

While Wyatt preferred to swim alone in the dark, quiet waters of his life, Tallulah was the socialite and center of the small community. She was their resident matchmaker. She had lived her entire life in one realm and knew everyone and their business. Just as he knew how to match his lure to the insects feeding the trout, Tallulah knew how to match couples. Expressions flashed through her eyes like lightning, especially threatening anger when he looked at Fallon and ached for her.

Fallon. She was the missing part of him; she'd been just a baby when her mother had fled, taking her away from him....

Wyatt flicked the lure's hackle with his finger again. After all these years of struggling to find and keep near Fallon and Miracle, to anonymously pay their bills and secure a safe life for them in rural Montana, he didn't intend to let one leggy, red-haired, volatile woman stand in his way....

Tallulah listened to the loose exhaust pipe of her small pickup truck rattle as she eased her way up the winding road to the lonely cabin. The canary yellow color was covered with road dust, which swirled inside the cab. Her fingers ached with tension and when she reached to smooth away the wave crossing her brow, her skin smelled like batter-fried onion rings. She'd prepared a huge batch for lunch while she'd mulled the bait that Wyatt Remington had dropped in her father's lap. Methodically separating the rings of an Idaho Sweet onion usually calmed her. She'd needed the relaxation before she faced Wyatt, a man as grim and dark and shabby as a battle-weary, lone timber wolf.

She slapped the catalog of W.R. Lures on the seat next to her.

Her onion therapy hadn't worked this time. Wyatt had dangled the lure successfully in front of her father. Then Mr. W.R. Lures had gently added the barb on his hook—he wanted to talk to Tallulah about her pie recipes. Wyatt admired her flaky crusts and wanted to learn how to bake them...*while* he was considering allowing her father to operate a world-famous W.R. Lure franchise within her father's small business. Because his business needed a boost,

Tallulah's father took the hook and ran with it—straight to her café. A franchise from W.R. Lures, with a daylong demonstration by the great Wyatt Remington, would boost sales. George Michaelson had licked the cherry-pie crumb from his lips, his eyes pleading with his daughter.

Tallulah gripped the steering wheel tighter as she muttered at a tiny meadow of flowers, "Pies...huh! He wants Fallon. Wyatt practically drools over her every time he sees her. And that bit about giving Miracle a toy or a children's book...that is just so he can get to Fallon, too! Well, he won't. Not if I have anything to say about it."

She glared at a doe and her fawn grazing in a clearing circled by pines. "You'll never get close to Fallon. You'll have to deal with me first, Mr. Franchise-dropper."

She scooped off her glasses, blew moisture on the big lenses and dried them on the hem of her shirt, tied into a knot under her breasts. She wanted no specks between her and Mr. Lure-man at the showdown.

She jammed on her glasses and brooded about what to do with Leroy, Wyatt's friend. She wasn't afraid to be alone with the two men in a remote cabin; her father knew exactly where she was going and when she would return. Wyatt didn't frighten her, despite his height, his broad shoulders and his tough, world-wise face.

She was too angry to be frightened. Mr. Ominous could try his looming with someone other than Fallon.

Leroy would have to step outside when the subject of Fallon arose.

"Creep," she mumbled at a chipmunk racing up a tree.

"Lech," she told the butterflies hovering over a glade of mountain daisies.

She jerked down the red bandanna securing her hair. Because she wanted Mr. Grim-and-Moody to know she was coming, Tallulah turned up the sound on her tape deck.

Chubby Checker's twisting music throbbed through the small pickup and Tallulah concentrated on maneuvering the small tires over the ruts that Wyatt's big pickup could manage easily. Her brakes screeched as she stopped next to Wyatt's gleaming dark blue power-packed monster, which had pulled his small silver trailer through town that first February day.

Everyone in Elegance had known the minute the superrig and aged, dented trailer had prowled through the only street in town. Actually, Main Street was a state highway, and the whole town had gotten wind of it within fifteen minutes after Denty Lang had rented the trailer hookup site to a Mr. Wyatt Remington.

Within an hour after he'd arrived, Wyatt had planted his hard backside on a café stool and had ordered Special Number Two—steak, potatoes, salad and green beans. Though clean, his clothing had seen better days. He looked like any other Westerner settling in the café for a meal—if you didn't notice the holes in his jeans, the fishing line securing a large tear, and the shabby sweatshirt with paint stains. His joggers were battered, the laces tied with frayed knots, and his windswept hair badly needed cutting.

The set of his jaw under his black beard was too hard, the lines etched around his grim mouth as if he'd lived on life's dark streets. He looked as though someone had tied him to a fence post and painted him with weather and hard times.

The first time she saw him gazing longingly at Fallon, as if all his dreams rested on Fallon's jumbled mass of dark-brown springy curls, as if he wanted to hold her in his arms—Tallulah didn't like the stranger.

Fallon was too vulnerable, just twenty-one and struggling to raise a three-year-old daughter. An anonymous relative's will had made her life easier. Her deceased benefactor had left her a tiny house in Elegance and a small income if she remained in the small, warm town. An attorney took care of the funds deposited in her name.

Fallon had lost a bit of her brittle, tight appearance. She remained lean and angular, her eyes dark and haunted below a mop of curls. She'd seen too much in her young life and didn't need one more problem—especially an older man who looked as though he'd been through the seven stages of Hell.

Wyatt coated himself with frost when the friendly locals tried to talk with him.

He acted unemployed—without a work schedule—patched his worn jeans with fishing line, though he *was an expert, world-class, trout fly-fishing-lure designer.*

Wyatt Remington's weathered skin did not present the image of a top sportsman, the owner of an exclusive fly-fishing-lure company.

Lately he had been glaring at her when she offered second pieces of pie to her customers.

Tallulah knew a good menacing glare when she saw one; she was famed for them. That was why she had been adding a blithe, cheery smile when she hustled Fallon away from him.

People said he was a drifter; they said he was a loner, down on his luck. He frequented the grocery store, the post office and the tiny washer-and-dryer room in the back of Maggie Crawford's Dry Goods store. Maggie thought the town should take up a collection for the stranger. She thought he didn't have enough money to get him to the next town or to a job. Theodora Monroe thought he was suffering from a broken heart; she had asked him to a church potluck dinner and had received a curt "Thanks. No."

Wyatt said little and looked a lot. Frost and dark clouds clung to him like a vampire's cape moving through the mist—

Tallulah allowed Chubby's overloud music to violate the area's silence a moment longer. Then she unlatched her fingers from her steering wheel. She briskly clicked the ignition off, noting the peaceful quiet surrounding the log cabin that concealed the infamous, leching, Fallon-desiring Mr. Wyatt Remington.

She hadn't told anyone her suspicions, because eventually a huge rumor would snowball and Fallon could be hurt.

Tallulah inhaled, pressed her lips together and slid her jeans-covered bottom out of the truck. She straightened her shoulders and knew that with the added height of her Western boots, she could face Wyatt Remington eyeball-to-eyeball.

She scowled at the cabin and the small ramp braced to one side of the steps as she walked toward it. Except for the longing when he looked at Fallon, Remington's eyeballs were guarded, sheathed by straight black lashes.

At thirty-eight, Tallulah had scores of matchmaking success stories behind her. She'd successfully matched most of her ex-boyfriends, because they really didn't suit her and deep down, she'd wanted them happy. Remington's black eyes, the grim set of his mouth and the gray hair sprinkled through his shaggy black waves didn't make a match with Fallon's honey brown, doelike eyes or her sweet, wounded youth.

Remington didn't take hints easily....

For the three months since he'd arrived, Tallulah had posted a big Hands Off sign on Fallon. Even Tallulah's ex-boyfriends knew better than to approach Fallon without Tallulah's permission, which she hadn't given. Yet Remington sprawled his length and his worn, denim backside on the café's stool one or two times a day and longed for Fallon; he tried to develop intimate little conversations with the girl and had once attempted a wistful, longing smile on his hard lips.

There wasn't a chance in the world those hard lips were touching Fallon's sweet ones.

Tallulah knocked at the cabin door. She hoped that Remington's friend, Leroy, was not of a gentle nature, because she didn't intend to pull her punches with Remington. She didn't want to emotionally scar a delicate soul with her kamikaze hit-and-run plan.

With luck, she could get Remington's prized franchise for her father's sporting-goods store *and* divert the master angler away from Fallon. Tallulah would be firm on the matter of Fallon and appealing in the area of winning the selective franchise. She would eyeball Wyatt into a sensible decision on both matters. . . .

A series of excited squeals and grunts sounded as Wyatt's deep voice rumbled out of the cabin. "Come in."

Taking a steadying breath and praying that she would not lose "the chance of a lifetime" her father needed very much, Tallulah opened the door.

Wyatt sat on a stool in a sunny corner of the gloomy cabin. Tallulah instantly resented his six-foot-four height and followed the length of his legs down to his Western boots.

She muttered a silent curse; she had looked forward to the eyeball scenario, leveling a glare at him. She knew she could be imposing when she wanted.

The May-afternoon sun outlined his lean body and Tallulah inhaled. In a black T-shirt and worn jeans, he looked lethal.

A series of grunts and bumps at her knee caused her to glance downward.

"Meet Leroy," Wyatt said, turning his attention back to the trash on the table in front of him.

"Leroy?" Tallulah repeated blankly as the pig's pink-and-black snout investigated her widely spread legs and her boots.

"Close the door. If he gets out, he'll make himself sick gorging on roots he shouldn't have," Wyatt murmured, bending closer to his task.

Tallulah slammed the door. "I'm here," she stated ominously.

"Uh-huh . . ." Wyatt returned in a slow, distant tone, his hands moving slowly on the table.

The pig gazed at her with beady eyes and bounced a small yellow ring on his snout. Tallulah noted that the animal needed to be on a diet; his stomach was too round. "Is this your friend?" she asked in her best threatening voice.

"Mmm."

"So... I'm here," she tried again, very patiently. When Wyatt continued studying the clutter in front of him, Tallulah inhaled sharply. She decided to pass on the matter of Wyatt's choice of friends and said in a careless tone, "My father tells me that you own W.R. Lures."

"Uh-huh."

Wyatt fitted something into a tiny vise and tightened it with practiced, concise movements. Tallulah slashed away the wonder that such large hands could fashion the delicate fly-fishing lures. She didn't want to admire anything about the man.

"He would like to carry the franchise on your lures. He said you dropped in and mentioned that you were *the* Wyatt Remington of W.R. Lures. You're a celebrity in the rod-and-reel business," she accused. Tallulah thought of her father's eyes gleaming with excitement, the lust for W.R.'s franchise riding him.

"So why did you want to talk with me about the possibility and pies?" she asked, leveling the straight-out question at Wyatt, who was poking through the table's colorful clutter with one finger.

Tallulah glanced at Leroy, who was looking at her expectantly and bouncing the ring on his snout. Instinctively she took the yellow ring, and Leroy swayed his potbelly a distance away from her. She tossed the ring gently into the air. The porker caught it neatly, grunted and trotted to her, a friendly smile pasted on his snout. She tossed the ring again, and when Leroy caught it, Wyatt pointed to a red rumpled rug.

The pig let out a squeal, but trotted to the rug, rooted it lovingly and plopped down on it. After staring at her for an instant, he picked up the leash and harness next to him in his mouth and bobbed it hopefully.

Tallulah supposed that Leroy was the best the somber drifter and expert angler could manage for friendship.

"If you're interested in baking pies, I'll kiss that pig," she told Wyatt, impatient to begin wrangling the real subject— Fallon.

When Wyatt slowly selected a tiny fluff and lifted it to the light, studying it and ignoring her, Tallulah added, "Don't you think it's a little dishonest—masquerading as an unemployed drifter, *when actually you own W.R. Lures?*"

She resented that her tone had risen during the last part of her sentence. Wyatt's broad shoulders lifted in a slow shrug.

"I'm talking to you," she said very quietly between her teeth.

Wyatt inclined his shaggy head toward a battered stool next to him. She hadn't seen him without his tattered denim jacket; the black T-shirt stretched tightly across his shoulders, and the cotton bulged over his upper arms, making him look tough.

The cords and muscles in his forearms moved beneath darkly tanned, hair-flecked skin.

Taking a deep, steadying breath, Tallulah walked to the stool and plopped down on it. She crossed her arms over her chest. She recognized the fly-tying equipment. "If you give my father the franchise, I'll teach you how to make pies. Meringue is my specialty—high and fluffy…. There, end of matter. Do we have an agreement or not?"

A small muscle in his cheek tightened. Wyatt carefully selected a feather from the table. Her fingers tightened on her arms. Wyatt's "clutter" was actually quite meticulous and orderly when she looked closer, just as deceptive as the man himself.

The tip of his forefinger strolled leisurely across the delicate feather.

The seductive movement caught Tallulah.

Something wrenched inside her and she tossed the feeling aside. She opened her mouth as Wyatt gently inserted a tiny hook into the vise and tenderly closed it. He stroked the hook lightly, lovingly, following it from barb to shank in an incredibly slow, sensual touch.

The movement of his big hands was erotic, graceful, hypnotic.

She remembered a movie in which a man's fingertips had prowled over a woman's naked skin—

Tallulah blinked, shaken by her thought. She inhaled and said, "My father's sporting-goods store really needs that franchise. If you demonstrated fly-casting techniques in the store while you're here, his business would pick up right away. The point is, *Mr.* Remington, he can't afford a high price tag. I thought if the price was within reach, I'd help him a bit. Just how much would W.R.'s franchise cost?"

Wyatt casually named a multithousand-dollar fee that caused her to gulp and shudder. Then he looked at her, the sunlight coming through the window, touching his high cheekbones and shadowing his cheeks. His jaw had the darkish cast of heavy beard.

"You've been married, haven't you?" he asked.

The question threw her off track. She brushed aside the uneasiness seeping over her along with the memory of Jack, her ex-husband. After twelve years, his accusations that their marriage would have worked if she hadn't been barren caught her each time she saw a child.

Wyatt was wrapping thread around dark hair, attaching it to a hook.

His long, lean, tapered fingers moved like a dancer, gliding closer to a lover, tantalizing—

Uh-huh, Tallulah thought. Right. A man with ballerina fingers. Somehow the idea fitted Wyatt, whom she considered a deceptive, lowdown skunk.... She inhaled quickly when she realized he was looking at her closely, his black eyes shielded as they traced her hair's side part. She watched those eyes roam across the deep wave to a nose laced with tiny freckles and a mouth too large and mobile to be sweet and feminine.

I am what I am, long and rangy, Tallulah thought unsteadily, as Wyatt continued his study down the length of her neck and across her shoulders. His gaze slid over her folded arms and down her legs before returning to the fly he was tying.

Tallulah shivered and refused to budge. She straightened her shoulders. He wasn't running her off until she had the matter of Fallon settled.

And, of course, the W.R. franchise attached to her father's sporting-goods store. She mulled over how to draw Wyatt out, to make him admit that he wanted Fallon. Then she would point out why he wasn't getting to the girl. There was one long, lean, tough reason: her.

Meanwhile, she watched Wyatt gently tug the hair on the lure upward, causing it to stand upright in miniature wings. He wiggled the wings with the very tip of his forefinger and Tallulah realized that her nipples had hardened beneath her crossed arms. Deep within her body the tiny clenching returned.

Her thighs quivered.

Wyatt caught a length of thread from the spool holder, sliding his fingers along it, and the gentlest moisture began to warm within Tallulah.

She swallowed abruptly. She recognized the sensual heat, and was shocked by it. She cleared her tightened throat and squirmed on the hard stool. "Wyatt..." Her voice came out husky and seductive.

Tallulah blinked again.

She caught Wyatt's underlying scents, the man-fragrance seductive beneath the soap. He probably only used fragrance-free products; sportsmen frequently disdained scents that would alert game. She delicately sniffed the exotic, tangy scent that was Wyatt's alone.

He cupped the tiny lure gently in his callused palm, studying the size and shape as though he were studying a woman's breast for contour and beauty.

"You're divorced and you're involved in everything in Elegance...you play volleyball on a mixed team..." Wyatt was saying softly, and Tallulah regretted her slight shiver.

"We have a team.... In the summer it will be softball. I've lived here all my life. I'm involved," Tallulah answered absently, because Wyatt had returned to gently plucking the tiny hairy wings of the lure.

"Uh-huh. You know everyone and you give second pieces of pie to your customers...even people passing through...say, truckers...tourists...almost everyone." Wyatt's deep voice had wrapped tightly around the last words.

She remembered instantly that she had never offered Wyatt a second slice of pie because of his drooling over Fallon...a young, vulnerable girl whom Tallulah was protecting until she had healed. "About the franchise..." Tallulah began instantly.

She noted Wyatt had added the perfected fly to a small orderly case. He tucked the case into a canvas vest with an assortment of pockets. When he stood slowly, Tallulah jumped off the chair and backed away a few steps. It was the first time she didn't have the protection of a counter between Wyatt and herself. His size suddenly alarmed her. Few men could loom over her.

Wyatt did loom over her, blocking out the sunlight, and a tiny quiver of excitement raced through her.

At least she wouldn't feel bad about warning off—and perhaps taking apart—a wimp. From the looks of Wyatt's size and fitness, she wouldn't have to worry about her conscience if she bruised his sensibilities.

She hated the flicker of amusement running through his hard eyes as he took off his battered T-shirt and tossed it onto the stool.

"I want to try out my new design," he said simply, and shrugged on the pocket-layered canvas vest. In seconds he had tugged on Leroy's harness and was walking out the door, Leroy's leash in one hand and a fly rod in the other.

The rhythm of her heart matched Leroy's hooves hitting the board ramp.

"Fine," she managed absently through a dry throat as she dealt with the image of a wide brown chest wedged by short, black curling hair.

"We'll just have our talk about lusting after Fallon outside," she said to the empty cabin. "You're in for it, Mr. W. R. Lure-maker. Because you are to keep away from Fallon."

She certainly wasn't interested in Wyatt herself—the tiny, quivery, sensual contractions she had experienced earlier were probably due to any number of things.

Say an overdose of Idaho Sweet onions or the bumpy road to the cabin.

Or impending middle age and the natural changes that occurred in a woman's body.

Tallulah closed her eyes. She had never seen anything so erotic in her life as Wyatt's big hands fashioning the tiny, delicate fly lure, plucking it, slowly, gently, into points.

She fearfully glanced down at her chest, where two nubs pressed against her cotton shirt. She rubbed the flat of her hand across her unsettled stomach, bared by the ends of the shirt tied under her chest, and followed Wyatt.

She decided that she'd settle the franchise and the matter of Fallon quickly; tomorrow the Tall Order Café would have another batch of deep-fried onion rings and everything in Elegance would settle down nicely.

Two

"So, we're agreed, then. You'll let my father have the franchise and make installments on it. Then at, say...oh, four o'clock every morning you'll come to the café for pie-baking lessons. But you'll have to keep up with me," Tallulah said as she skipped a stone across the stream.

Wyatt inhaled sharply; rule number one of accompanying a fisherman was not to make noise. She had been stalking on the bank behind him, crashing through the weeds and tossing her master plan at him. She finished with a tone that said her counteroffer was too reasonable to be dismissed.

Her tone also said that she didn't think Wyatt would come to the Tall Order's back door at four o'clock in the morning.

Tallulah was proving to be predictable, Wyatt thought. He cast with his right hand, then expertly played the line—drawing in, tugging it, mimicking an insect's flight—with his left one. In constant movement, she planned everything around her and assumed that others agreed with her; she steamrollered the entire town with second slices of pie and sympathy—of course, her plans were always for the benefit of others.

A red-haired whirlwind, moving so quickly that nothing could catch her.

He would; he was a patient man. Wyatt flicked a high-riding fly over the surface of the winding, small stream. The rippling, fish-stocked water was one of the reasons he had chosen Elegance for the home of his daughter and grand-daughter. The stream offered multiple conditions needed to properly test a new fly design.

From the bank, he could flick the fly upstream to rough water and allow it to ride downstream with the rest of the hatching insects. He concentrated on the elements of the dry fly working the stream, on the hatching insects flying low over the water, and on the woman who was trashing the woodland peace like an elephant on a rampage.

Wyatt considered how her eyes had latched to his chest when he'd stripped the T-shirt away. He'd done it automatically; he liked to fish with the vest alone, his casting arm unhampered by clothing.

Behind her huge lenses, Tallulah had stared at his chest in a way that caused a man's ego to rise about ten stories. He hadn't been prepared for his reaction, the need to unknot her blouse from beneath those high breasts and fit her against him very carefully.

He wondered who took care of Tallulah, when she was so busy taking care of everyone else. Including a horde of ex-boyfriends, their wives and girlfriends.

"You haven't caught anything yet," Tallulah called impatiently, and Leroy squealed from his tether to a pine tree.

Wyatt pressed his lips together and realized that he had miscast, snapping his forearm forward a little too late. "I'm considering it," he said above the sound of the gurgling water.

"I haven't got all day," she grumbled, walking down to the rocky shoreline beside him.

"Get back from my casting arm," Wyatt ordered grimly.

Tallulah glared at him, but moved to his other side. She watched the lure drifting down the stream. "It can't be that hard."

What was hard was very hard, Wyatt brooded as he watched the fly float on the water and locked his knees against the sensual needs rising sharply within him.

A very careful, controlled man who traveled constantly, Wyatt had his last sexual experience years ago. He tried to give a part of his heart to Grace and failed. He couldn't ask her to settle for less than happiness, and had decided that he couldn't give it to her.

When Tallulah had arrived at the cabin, a nuance of eau de onion clinging to her, she had stood and planted her booted feet apart in the doorway like a Western gunslinger. The sunlight had glinted on her red-gold hair and outlined the slender curved length of her long legs, her gently rounded hips and her narrow waist. Wyatt had admired those long legs as she'd jitterbugged with her ex-boyfriends in the Tall Order Café. He had awakened during the past few weeks from dreams of those long legs wrapped around his waist and holding him tightly, after which he was offered second pieces of pie. The mixed scenario unbalanced him just as much as Tallulah—

Her scent—once he bypassed the onion aroma—was the essence of femininity, heady with musk and lightened with bath powder and soaps. Tallulah was a very natural woman who used few cosmetics.

It wasn't that she was beautiful; she wasn't. Tallulah's jaw ran a little to the strong side, and one half of her face didn't exactly match the other half. The left corner of her mouth lifted in a wide grin more quickly than the right side, but her right cheek hid a tiny dimple. Tiny lines around her eyes deepened when she smiled—at other people. Her wardrobe ran to sweaters or T-shirts and jeans.

She was what he admired most in an opponent—a tough fighter—and he admired her protection of his daughter. In fact, he was grateful for it.

"I want you to stop watching Fallon," Tallulah was saying in a distracted tone as she observed the methodical whip of his line over the glistening stream.

"Fallon?" Wyatt cast automatically, concentrating on the woman beside him.

"Uh-huh. She's young and sweet. You're not. You're not a good match," Tallulah answered in an absent tone as she scanned the stream. "Why don't you cast over there?"

Every muscle and nerve in Wyatt's body tightened as he mentally shifted from Tallulah's long-legged, leanly curved body to whatever she was saying now. "A good match?"

He missed setting the hook in a rainbow trout. It had surged out near the cattails on the opposite side of the bank. Wyatt cast again, whipping the line over the sunlit surface.

"Not a good match," Tallulah was saying, eyeing the lure as it rode the water. "Keep away from her."

Wyatt's arm stopped in midcast and the line plopped into the stream. He clamped his lips against the curse wanting to burst out of him. Tallulah thought that he was after his own daughter!

He was, damn it! After he'd searched most of Fallon's lifetime and found her just two years ago, Tallulah wasn't keeping him away from the relationship he ached to have with his family. She wasn't interfering with the safety he would provide for them.

"You haven't caught anything," she reminded him shortly while he chewed on this latest bit of news and tried to keep the smoothness in his casts.

"Exactly why don't you like me?" he asked carefully, and sensed Tallulah's smoky gray eyes staring up at him.

"You're ogling a girl half your age or younger. Fallon is vulnerable now...you could hurt her beyond repair," Tallulah stated flatly. "Even if there wasn't an age gap, you're not matchmaking material."

Wyatt inhaled unevenly and continued flicking the fly over the water, deliberately avoiding the two big trout that leaped out of their dark homes to take the lure. He didn't want distraction, not even a record trout, when he dealt with the nooks and crannies of Tallulah's mind.

Her bent mind, he added, as he continued flicking the line.

"That doesn't look so hard," she said beside him.

Wyatt reacted instantly. He dropped the line he had been holding in his left hand and reached for Tallulah's shirt, gripping it and hauling her up to him. He lowered his face to her unyielding one.

He studied her dark gray, stormy eyes. Then he realized with horror that he had never jerked another woman to him.

Or wanted one as desperately.

Or was infuriated as quickly as he had just been by Miss Tallulah Ames.

He forced his fingers to uncurl from her shirt and she tugged it down briskly. Her generous lips were trimmed with a grim satisfaction because she had gotten to him.

"See?" she asked smugly. "You're not proper matchmaking material. It's written all over you."

Wyatt forced his smile and handed her his fishing rod. Concentrating on Tallulah would require more than keeping his hands busy with the rod. He wanted to study her, circle her and drive her nuts for a change. "You try it. After all, it doesn't look so difficult to do, does it?"

Her reddish curls tossed in the sunlight as she shook her head. "Not a bit. Dad showed me how when I was a little girl. Of course, I realize you must *try* to make it look difficult to make yourself look good and to sell lures. Unlike you, I can concentrate on a task and carry on a conversation, too," she said, then frowned instantly and clamped her lips closed.

The line and hook sailed past Wyatt's ear to catch a pine cone. Tallulah tugged sharply and Wyatt closed his eyes and asked quietly, "Have you been fishing recently, Tallulah?"

She glared at him as the pine cone sailed into the water, falling free with the lure. Wyatt studied the lureless line whipping out in the ripple and asked, "What else don't you like about me? Other than the fact I'm not matchmaking material... and we'll pick that topic up later."

The line tangled in the cattails and Tallulah fought like a master angler until she extracted one, roots and stalk. "Repeat...anyone can do this easily," she stated with a note of triumph.

There was nothing like the uplifted curve of Tallulah's breast as she cast, Wyatt was thinking as he admired the long feminine curves next to him. In the dappled sunlight, her hair was the color of aspens, golds and oranges and shimmering silvers. She had the clean, clear look of a confident woman who knew herself well.

Tallulah concentrated on playing the hookless line. "You're misleading... like letting Dad think Leroy was human—your friend at the cabin. And leading people to think you're unemployed and down on your luck— Maggie was all for taking up a collection for you. And you looking at Fallon like some lovesick boy just waiting for a tiny bit of attention and playing up to Miracle, just to get close to Fallon. When all the time you were Mr. W. R. Lures himself.... Now, I ask you, don't you catch a bit of dishonesty in this picture?"

She frowned, leaned forward and concentrated on the trout that was staring in the hookless line. "Come on...take it...take it, big guy. Yum."

Then, in a low, intent tone, she said, "You live like a gypsy, Mr. Remington. Dad told me how you travel around the country, sometimes overseas, putting on demonstra-

tions and selling your lures. Fallon needs strength and a
home and safety and she needs to be wrapped in love that
isn't . . . isn't with a man who will someday decide to move
his camper on down the road. . . . Ah! Look at that big one,
would you? Come to Mama!''

"So you've been protecting Fallon from a lusty old son
of a buck who isn't fit matchmaking material and who will
probably leave when he's ready. Is that how you read me,
Tallulah?''

She tugged the line with her free hand. "Dented camper
trailer and all. You've got road dust written all over you.
You've got the picture. . . . Look at the size of that one.''

"Water magnifies," Wyatt said flatly after glancing at the
trout looking at the empty line.

"Don't get miffed because fly fishing isn't that hard and
because you're not suitable matchmaking material for Fallon or any other woman. Some guys just aren't.''

Wyatt studied the taut denim over Tallulah's backside. He
studied the shape of her intently, and decided that she would
fit his palm very neatly. "I could be.''

Her "Huh" was flat and disbelieving. "It would take
work. For one thing, Fallon deserves a truly romantic man,
a partner who is fun loving, Mr. Remington. Leching isn't
loving. I've seen you every day since February . . . maybe
twice a day. You're a loner and you don't laugh. People get
frostbite from you.''

She was getting to him, Wyatt admitted, chafed by the
dour picture Tallulah had painted. He remembered all the
temporary jobs he'd taken while tracing Fallon, traveling to
Europe and across Canada; he remembered all the hours
spent trying to develop the business and marketing it, the
personal appearances and guide trips with wealthy sports
enthusiasts and outdoor-magazine writers. There were other
hours spent calling and following clues about his daughter
and fitting in short trips to wherever someone thought he
had seen her. He'd traveled and worked and there'd been

little time for anything else, because more than anything he wanted to provide for his daughter.

Two years ago, he'd finally located Fallon, who had run away from her mother. Wyatt had moved carefully, aware that he could lose Fallon too easily. When he began asking questions about her, the answer was ugly: "Her old man? Her mom told her that her father is some bozo who beat up her mother all the time. So her mom took off as soon as she could. Her mother is a witch and had a boyfriend who hit on Fallon. Fallon hates her old man, though she hasn't ever seen him. Said she doesn't want to ever see him."

He'd never touched Michelle, his ex-wife, in any way but that of a hot-blooded youth hungry for the girl he loved. *Loved.* At twenty-two, he had confused sex with love for Michelle and they were married in a storybook wedding. Michelle didn't like housework, bills or staying home with a new baby. Fallon had arrived in their first year of marriage and Michelle had wanted a divorce. Once the papers were in her hand, she left the slow-moving, small Georgia town with their baby and kept moving for years.

From the threads he'd pieced together of Fallon's life, Wyatt knew she'd never had safety or a childhood. As a young teenager, Fallon had tried for love and had gotten pregnant by a neighborhood Romeo out for fun. Miracle was just a year old when Wyatt found Fallon and Miracle in a New York slum.

An attorney instantly set up the funds—a bogus inheritance from some lost relative who loved Elegance and wanted Fallon to settle in it. The "inheritance" would allow Fallon and Miracle to travel to and live in the town Wyatt had investigated and considered safe. Where he could enter their lives gently.

Until now, Tallulah had prevented him from having a relationship with Fallon . . . because Tallulah considered him too old, too grizzled, too unfit for matchmaking. . . .

He leaned aside as the line whizzed by his shoulder and braced himself as Tallulah enticed another cattail stalk to her. "Take it easy," he muttered, and realized he meant not only taking care of the line, but relaxing her assault on his ego.

Wyatt felt delicate and wounded.

He groaned slightly as he recognized the new emotions and Tallulah frowned at him.

"Sorry," she said briefly. "Do you think I should change the fly? They don't seem to want this one. You have to match the hatch, you know. Whatever insects are hatching along the stream, you need to choose a fly that looks like them— Goodness, what a dark frown! Are we in a mood, Mr. W. R. Lures?"

Wyatt jerked a box of lures from his vest pocket and thrust it into Tallulah's hand. She clamped the rod between her thighs, holding it; delicately fashioned muscles surged beneath her jeans. Wyatt began to sweat despite the cool May afternoon and stripped off his vest, dropping it onto a large rock. He glanced uneasily at the neatly lined flies in the foam-layered box that were being dislodged by Tallulah's rampaging fingers.

He glanced back at the rod between her thighs and closed his eyes. To discover his own fly had problems after more years than he could easily count unnerved him. "Do you need any help... selecting a fly?"

"I'm fine," Tallulah said as the delicate tip of Wyatt's best-loved rod ground into the rocks.

"Oh, hell. Give me that," he said, gripping the rod and tugging it from between her thighs. "So you consider me a romantic reject?"

"Mr. Dreamboat you aren't," Tallulah said distantly as she concentrated on tying the knot in the thin line.

Wyatt noted that the childish knot could be unraveled with the slightest tug of the stream, but he didn't want to be distracted from Tallulah.

"Lessons might help," he said quietly as Tallulah took the rod and sailed the lure out into the stream.

"I don't need lessons. I'm fine," she said, watching the line.

Wyatt gripped the back of her waistband as she stepped out onto a large rock in the stream. He'd tried that rock and it had teetered with his weight. "So if I promise to keep my leching away from Fallon, do you think you might give me lessons so that I'd be choice Grade A matchmaking material?"

"No way. I'm a busy woman, Wyatt. Molding you into romantic material would take too much time."

"Make time," he ordered grimly.

Her snort was delicate and disbelieving. "Let's get back to the matter of the franchise. Pie-making skills bartered for Dad's installments on the W.R. Lures franchise."

"Wrong."

The rock teetered as Tallulah turned to him, the sunlight glinting on her hair and on her lenses. "I hope I heard you wrong," she warned tightly.

"I want to be romantically appealing matchmaking material. You're going to give me lessons in exchange for my backing of your father's store, a W.R. Lures franchise and demonstration lessons from a master angler," Wyatt said darkly, glaring at her and locking his fingers tighter on her waistband. Somewhere in his logical galaxy, another Wyatt stood and *tsk-tsked* at this new unstable, unmethodical, emotional Wyatt.

Tallulah glared at him, then turned back and began casting again. She balanced on the teetering rock. "Not a chance. I'm short on time."

Wyatt jerked her jeans waistband just as she cast into the chokecherry bushes beside him. The hook caught in the branches as Tallulah pivoted gracefully off the shifting rock and leaped to the bank, on the other side of Wyatt. Strung between the bushes and Tallulah, who was rubbing his best rod in the mud, Wyatt found his body quickly looped in the fishing line.

He turned just as the line tangled around Tallulah's ankles and he caught her on his way down the grassy, flower-splashed bank. Tallulah rolled across him, and where the bank slanted, he rolled over her and the line tangled them securely together.

Tallulah lay under Wyatt, stunned at the fast tumble. His cheek lay aside hers, and he appeared to have had the wind knocked from him. "Are you all right?" she whispered when he didn't move.

She swallowed and breathed quietly and realized how heavy he was. If he was unconscious, it was up to her to save them. The stream was only a few yards away and if they rolled into the water— She blinked and swallowed again and squirmed, pushing at his chest with her hands, and found her fingers latching on to warm hair. He grunted and inhaled just as they slid slightly and she rolled over on him, entangling them in another round of line.

They rolled over once more, ending up with Wyatt's body over hers. "I'm fine. Just dandy. If you'll hold still, I'll get us out of this," Wyatt muttered, and turned his head to look down their tangled bodies. He stilled, his eyes dark and intent as they slowly traveled down their bodies.

Tallulah heard his breath whoosh by her ear when she tried to squirm out from under him. "Don't panic," Wyatt said very softly, and she realized distantly that his tone was laced with a Southern drawl. His hand moved up her side to test the line running across her hips; it flattened momentarily over her bottom, and for a disbelieving instant before his fingers moved away, Tallulah thought he might have squeezed her bottom.

"Just lie still," he began patiently, "until I can find—"

He inhaled sharply, the movement pressing his chest against her softness. "If you lie still, we can get free more quickly," he offered in a too-reasonable tone, rather like an adult reasoning with a child.

"Don't worry. I'm agile," she returned, offended at his "male playing me-strong, you-helpless-woman" tone. She'd taken care of herself and everyone else ever since she could remember; she had inherited the role from her mother, who'd passed away when Tallulah was eleven.

They slid down a few inches on the bank and Wyatt's hand shot out to grip a bush, anchoring them for the moment.

"Now you've done it," Wyatt snapped. "Leave it to a red-haired, interfering, long-legged whirlwind to—" he cursed, and ordered, "Stop wiggling, Tallulah."

Tallulah realized that Wyatt was a very aroused man, with his heart beating rapidly and his temperature rising. She glanced at the dark heat of his eyes and traced the flush rising in his cheeks. His body under hers was very hard and warm. Tallulah squirmed, trying to wiggle free of the line, and they rolled once more, and Wyatt lay over her. He scowled down at her. "I am trying to save you," she explained carefully to him.

"Oh, hell," he muttered in the tone of a captain going down with his ship.

Then Wyatt Remington, master angler, placed his mouth precisely over hers. With a butterfly caress, he smoothed the contours of her lips with his. He paused in the sensitive corners and Tallulah shivered; until now, that particular geography of her mouth had been virginal—unkissed.

She stared up at him through her dirtied lenses, saw the intense expression drawing his eyebrows together, as his hand framed her cheek to lift her mouth to his.

She found herself taking his bait—those delicate little caresses from his hard mouth.

Tallulah had never been kissed so sweetly, so exactly, so perfectly. She sighed, allowing her lids to flutter shut. She opened them when she felt her glasses being drawn from her.

Because she felt exposed as she had never been, even with her ex-husband, Tallulah rummaged for a verbal sword. "We're trapped in *your* fishing line," she accused as the sunlight touched Wyatt's head, glistening and catching blue lights in the black, wayward strands.

"Uh-huh," he said, looking down at her carefully.

Tallulah squirmed a bit, flushing beneath his inspection. She wondered distantly when anyone had looked at her this closely, as if he were looking into her soul.

Something flickered in her and she saw more pain and loneliness than anyone should bear. She ached for him, wanting to soothe him—

He closed his eyes slowly and frowned. Then he carefully eased his hard body nearer to hers, as if he was fitting himself for a lifetime relationship. A soft, intimate, masculine growl slid around the coils of her ear, entered her feminine senses and pleased her very much. She didn't have time to debate him as a romantic reject. He was kissing her again, and this time she wrapped her arms around his neck and held tight. Just for this moment, here while they were trapped on this sunlit, earth-scented, flower-studded bank, Tallulah wanted to keep Wyatt safe and warm from whatever haunted him. She locked him to her and kissed him with one-hundred-percent tender delight.

"Mmm." He gathered her closer and deepened the kiss. He slanted his mouth over hers with the same deliberate care as he had fitted the length of his body to hers.

She started to tremble, and searched for the reason before she pushed everything away but the sweetness of his kiss. She smelled his hair, his skin, the heat of him. His shoulders rippled when she smoothed them gently, and she answered the tentative flick of his tongue against her lips with her own.

"Mmm," he murmured appreciatively again, then stroked the back of her neck with his fingers as he bent to whisper in her ear—when he wasn't nibbling on the lobe or flicking his tongue gently against the whorls.

She trembled and heated and wondered why no man had treated her ears to such delight. She saw the tiny lure dangling from the chokecherry bushes and remembered his fingers plucking the fly's miniature wings and stroking them gently. Tiny muscles within her contracted immediately. She dug her fingers into the strong muscles of his back, needing to latch herself to reality. She had been married and had boyfriends, and...

"Kiss your toes and the backs of your knees..." Wyatt was saying huskily, his chest vibrating against her breasts.

Tallulah stared up at the blue sky and melted as Wyatt murmured ways he'd like to please her and taste her, all in a Southern drawl. After a soft gasp and a delicate explosion, she closed her eyes and lay in a breathless, limp, heated pool beneath him.

Wyatt stroked her stomach, her hips, and soothed her cheek with his hot one. Though he shuddered above her, keeping his full weight away, he seemed reluctant to release her, and placed his angular, flushed face in the curve of her throat, resting upon her.

She smoothed his back as he shuddered again and kissed her damp throat and nuzzled her cheek. "Tallulah," he said slowly, softly, as if fitting the name to his lips.

Then he began to carefully unwind the line from them. She wanted to scramble free. Instead she lay beneath his weight, absorbing the look and scent of this new Wyatt and trying to pull her melted body back together.

Minutes later, Tallulah glared at the pig that had slept through the entire scene and that now watched her flushed face with beady eyes. She dusted her bottom and straightened her blouse while Wyatt methodically reeled in his line and eyed her.

She looked away from his slightly swollen mouth and tried not to think about what it had whispered in her ear.

She looked at the iridescent trout arcing out of the water after an insect, then she looked at the pig, which looked back.

She cleared her throat and forced her unsteady legs to lock at the knee. "Well. Well," she said again, more briskly than the first time. "Isn't this a nice day?"

"Sure is," Wyatt said huskily after a long pause.

Tallulah glanced over his head at the soaring birds. Then she swallowed and took the glasses that Wyatt handed her and shoved them on to her nose.

She blew away a leaf from her left lens and stated carefully, "I cannot abide a lech, especially one who grabs every woman in sight when he can't have the one he's been drooling over."

Wyatt's eyebrows jammed together. He slowly placed the pole against a tree and put his hands in his back pockets. "What?"

"You heard me. You think that here we are, all lined up on a shelf and ready to go. All ages, all sizes. You'll grab any woman in sight," Tallulah repeated, her anger rising. He wasn't unemployed, wasn't penniless and wasn't all that cold natured. At least when he kissed and settled himself upon her. She remembered his hard, intimate outline, which remained quite obvious as he stood, legs locked and apart. To her horror, she glanced at him and flushed.

"You think that if I can't get Fallon, I'll take you?" Wyatt asked in a soft tone that grew loud and indignant, frightening a chipmunk that scurried across the clearing. He jerked one hand from his back pocket, ran it through his shaggy hair and scowled at her. His hand rubbed the hair on his chest as he continued glaring at her.

"That's about the size of it," she informed him, and began looking at the bank for the path back to the cabin.

"Stay here and fight," Wyatt snapped.

"Can't. Have to get back to the Tall Order. We're adding another special—cabbage rolls."

"Tallulah," Wyatt shouted as she dashed up the embankment. "I said, stay put."

Leroy snorted and scrambled to his feet, staring at Wyatt, then at Tallulah and back again.

She turned on Wyatt with a slow, triumphant smile. An expert in her people-sensing skills, she'd drawn out the worst in him and scored a point for her cause. "You yelled at me. That really is unacceptable in proper matchmaking material. You're a regular Gothic hero, Mr. W. R. Lures. Too emotional. Right now you're rolling in angst. You're too set in your ways to change. In short...you're a very unmarketable male. Gothic guys are out of mode."

Sensing that the showdown was reaching its climax, Leroy started squealing. A yellow flower, dislodged by his foraging, bobbed on his snout. Tallulah had the odd sense that the porker was enjoying a spectator sport, that he was encouraging her, rooting for her and waving his own special flag.

Down by the stream, Wyatt breathed quietly, as though trying to control himself. The sun caught the slow, determined rise and fall of his chest, and his fingers curled and released, then he said, "Lady, I never yell. You're a bossy, small-town, small-minded busybody. What you need is a man who will stand up to you and won't be handed off when you decide to fix him up with someone else.... You've got a track record of doing just that."

His dark eyes roamed down her body, heating it again, then back up to the glasses she had just straightened. Her angry shudder had dislodged them. She wanted to launch herself down the embankment and push him into the freezing water. "Stay away from Fallon," she said between her teeth.

"I never figured you for a coward or a tease," he returned quietly as he picked up his rod, turned and began casting. The rigid set of his shoulders defied her.

He caught a brown trout instantly, reeled it in and released it. He repeated the scenario three times in just as many minutes.

Three

Tying lures usually relaxed him, but after an encounter with Tallulah his mind was locked on long legs and sweet, hungry kisses, Wyatt had discovered by three o'clock the next morning. He closed his "makings" box and sighed. Leroy watched him anxiously, as though worried about Wyatt's strange new restlessness, which was noticeable in the tiny camper. He slid a Miss Swine tape into the video player, and while Leroy grunted appreciatively, Wyatt thought about the contrary Tallulah.

While he couldn't tell her about Fallon just yet, he wasn't slackening his line to reel her in. She'd taken the bait and run with it.

"'Gothic guy,'" he repeated darkly. Wyatt rubbed Leroy's bristly back. Sharing female problems with the little porker provided a measure of therapy.

Wyatt thought about Tallulah's assortment of exboyfriends and found himself scowling at the television's delectable Miss Swine. In the three months that he had been in Elegance, he'd gotten a picture of Tallulah's romantic life from the assortment of men who frequented the café. Jimmy Folton had held his wife close as they'd slow-danced to the jukebox's music and had joked with Tallulah as she passed carrying platters of burgers and fries. "Hey, babe. Aren't you sorry you broke our engagement now and let this pretty little sweetheart have me?"

Tex Marshall had jogged into the café with his girlfriend for breakfast and teased, "Some women don't know a good man. When you threw me back, Stretch, my little Angel grabbed me. Your loss."

Tallulah's revolving romances were recalled with light humor, such as Linc Jones's comment, "You were right, Stretch. Melanie does kiss better than you."

The memories were a part of Elegance's historical fabric, flowing around the Tall Order like melted butter on pancakes. Tallulah glowed when she looked at the couples she had matched. Apparently one or two of the men had to be coached in the romantic pursuit of their ladyloves. Netty Wilson had thanked Tallulah for suggesting her boyfriend order African violets as a gift. Georgina Ramsey loved the tiny locket that Alfred gave her the romantic night he asked her to be his "steady girl."

"'Romantic reject...unsuitable matchmaking material,'" Wyatt repeated darkly as Leroy snorted lustily after Miss Swine, who was reclining in a mud bath.

Wyatt didn't want to think about how Tallulah had kissed the men in her past. He hadn't kissed a woman for years, and when he fitted his mouth over Tallulah's, he'd had a sense of coming home. Her hair had smelled like sunshine and...onions, Wyatt admitted truthfully as he smiled slightly.

When he thought of her gripping his back and holding him tight, of the earth-and-flower scents tangling with Tallulah's, something tore in Wyatt and he shifted uneasily.

"'Road dust,'" he muttered, nettled by her reference to his traveling life and "dented camper."

He rose slowly, stretched and looked out into the moon-lit Montana night. He was suddenly very weary, the years weighting him as he tugged open a refrigerator that housed assorted plastic tubs of grubs and worms instead of Sunday leftovers and the makings for a backyard barbecue.

He wanted to give Fallon a home, make her life easier, and to share Miracle. He planned to move so slowly, to enter her life so gently, that Fallon would know how much he loved her.

Had always loved her, from the first moment he saw her. Wyatt cleared his suddenly tight throat and inhaled shakily to steady his emotions. He thought of all the nights he wondered where she was. Was she safe? Was she happy? Did she have enough to eat and was she warm?

Fallon. Too thin and pale, her face almost covered by jumbled curls, she had lost a little of her fearful look in the two years she'd lived in the town. From her letters to Wyatt's attorney, she was making her first home and Miracle was thriving. She was safe in Elegance with her long-legged, red-haired watchdog standing guard.

He'd been having the restaurant's February chili when Tallulah had pressed her hand to Fallon's forehead. Within minutes, she had bundled his daughter in her coat and sent her home with a jar of chicken-noodle soup and the offer to keep Miracle overnight.

He'd had good evidence that Fallon was well protected from irresponsible suitors.

He should have been around in her early teens to keep her safe....

Wyatt squeezed his eyes shut as another wave of pain hit him. Lord, how he wanted to hold his daughter against him, to cuddle his granddaughter on his lap and rock her to sleep. To wrap them both in safety.

In the shadowy mirror over the refrigerator, the years haunted his bearded face, lodging in grim lines, a scar near his temple, gray catching the dim light. "Mr. Gothic Guy," he muttered.

Wyatt closed the door and eased into bed, folding his arms behind him and thinking about Tallulah. He'd dealt with loneliness for years, and never was the tug so sharp as when he'd forced himself away from her.

He hadn't meant to kiss her, but her wiggling had worsened his desire. Poignant, fully aching, his need for her had surged out of the years of abstinence. She tasted like everything he'd missed, like everything he'd ever wanted— She held him tight, as if she was protecting him, keeping him safe.

He glanced at Leroy, who was too absorbed in Miss Swine to notice Wyatt's loneliness. It was nice that one male in the camper wasn't lonely, anyway.

Tallulah looked at the bouquet and then at the man peering over the florist's red roses at her—Wyatt Remington. Seated at the counter, he wore a tight smile and a clean, but rumpled cotton shirt, a change from his usual sweatshirt or T-shirt.

Tallulah almost dropped the armload of breakfast plates she was carrying to the truckers' table. When she came back after serving the men, Wyatt was still watching her over the roses. She hastened Louise away—the waitress had been filling the condiments and dropping soda crackers in the sugar to keep it dry. With Louise's gaze locked on Wyatt, the sugar had spilled onto the counter, and Tallulah wiped it hastily as she scowled at him.

He studied the loose curls perched on top of her head and the tendrils at her forehead and down her nape. For an instant Tallulah's heart paused, and then it raced madly as Wyatt's gaze touched her lips and she remembered their kiss.

Their kiss, because she had held him just as tightly and kissed him back just as fervidly. There they were, tangled in fishing line, oblivious to the grass stains she later found on her back, kissing the very juices out of each other on a sunny bank by the stream like two hungry teenagers.

No one had kissed her like that. Not ever. Not even her ex-husband.

As if Wyatt needed her to survive.

As if only he knew the secret of her lips' sensitive virginal corners.

Since Wyatt was her sworn foe, the kissing scene was a bit shattering. She must have been high on the scent of onions when she'd responded to Mr. W. R. Lures.

"What do you want?" she snapped at him, shooing a wide-eyed Fallon along with a gentle flick of her towel.

Wyatt's lips lifted to bare his teeth slightly. "Lessons. Bring me up to par. Take me out of the romantic-reject lane."

"Huh. First it's meringue and then it's romance," she muttered disbelievingly, scooping the last of the spilled sugar into her hand and dumping it in the trash. She whizzed by him to tuck her written order into the cook's revolving wheel. She turned, took a second look at the roses, jammed her ordering pad into her belt and mumbled, "You look weird, Remington."

"I put on after-shave," he stated defensively, the roses trembling in his fist.

Unable to resist, Tallulah bent to nuzzle them.

"These are for you," Wyatt said tightly. "I thought of them by myself," he added after a moment. "I can wire my partner to start the franchise process if you agree to upgrade me to matchmaker material."

Tallulah studied him to see if he was glancing woefully at Fallon, but his eyes remained locked with hers, dark and burning. "Oh," she said airily, taking the roses from him and hurrying into the kitchen.

She ran water into a vase while she watched Wyatt through the cook's window. She ordered his usual breakfast of steak and eggs and studied the comb marks in his shaggy black hair and the new shaving cut on his jaw, and a jaw which moved as though he was gritting his teeth.

Norm, her day cook, groaned and rubbed his ample belly. He looked at her grimly as she gently arranged her very first rose bouquet in the vase. "Wasn't my cooking that's making me sick," he muttered, flipping over a short stack of pancakes into a plate and handing them to her. "No, you are not sticking a thermometer in my mouth or shoving a handful of vitamin C down my gullet," he added firmly when she began to hover around him. "I'll let you know if I don't feel well enough to work."

"Make sure you do." She picked up the side order of hash-brown potatoes and dry toast on her way out and stopped to meet Wyatt's grim stare. She grabbed a coffee-pot in her free hand and sailed to the Parkers' booth to warm their coffee. Then she noticed Fallon smiling shyly at Wyatt, who was looking like an orphan pup as he stared into his coffee.

If ever there was a look that would grab a woman, it was that orphan-pup look that some men wore; that "I need petting and a good home" look would fill any woman's heart with the need to cuddle and comfort. A really good orphan-pup look—like the one Wyatt wore—was more potent than any romantic dash and charm. Tallulah eyed Wyatt and decided he deserved the prize—even she, who knew he'd take any woman within grabbing distance, wanted to cuddle him. She'd gotten a whiff of his loneliness when he stretched himself over her, and she'd held him tightly to keep him safe.

But she had no time to waste, because Fallon had paused at his stool and was smiling gently at him.

The look that passed between the older man and the girl sizzled Tallulah's insides. Especially when Wyatt's black eyes lit up like the Fourth of July. Fallon's honey brown eyes were warming— "Fallon, the corner table wants a high chair for the baby and Mr. Jones needs a coffee refill. Take care of it for me, will you? Then make another couple of pots of coffee, because those truckers want another round. They're waiting for some old boy driving a cattle truck."

Wyatt's eyes lingered on the girl as she moved away, and Tallulah inhaled. She nodded toward the kitchen. "You. In the kitchen."

"Yes, ma'am," Wyatt said slowly, unwinding his length from the stool and bringing his coffee with him.

Beneath his cook's white hat, Norm looked at her with big, shadowed woeful eyes and rubbed his stomach as he flipped an order of hash browns and turned a sausage patty. While Tallulah glared up at Wyatt and furiously tore washed lettuce into a huge plastic tub, he scanned the shining grills, the ovens, the fry cookers and the neat arrangement of gallon cans and foods on the huge shelves.

Wyatt sipped his coffee and watched with interest as Tallulah bashed a head of lettuce against the cutting board and cut out its core as though it were his heart. She usually removed the core by pulling it with her fingers, but she wanted to make a definite point with Wyatt. He lifted an eyebrow as she opened her mouth and closed it.

"You will not," she began, "look at Fallon as if something is passing between you that no one else can share."

"Oh? Give me one reason why not," he said as she ripped the lettuce apart and threw it into a huge colander to be washed.

"I told you. You're not a good match." Tallulah inhaled and caught a whiff of his after-shave. She backed up two feet when he straightened and looked down at her with dark, exciting interest. Or was it humor?

Her heart started thumping faster and she felt a little dizzy.

"I'm sick," Norm stated flatly, and handed Wyatt his spatula. "Somebody take over. Going home... Two looking up at you," he said, referring to eggs that were not turned over. "Short stack, spuds, dry toast. Rolls raising."

Then he walked out of the kitchen and the café. He stopped at the door and yelled back to Tallulah, "Tour bus pulling into the parking lot. Maybe twenty people. They look hungry." And then he was gone.

"Give me that," Tallulah muttered, and was unable to take the spatula from Wyatt's hand. He walked to the hook holding clean aprons and tied one around his waist.

Wyatt expertly poured pancakes, shoveled frozen hash browns onto the grill and scraped away the crumbs from the grill's last order of French toast. He flipped the pancakes, reached for another sheet of orders that Fallon had just placed on the cook's wheel, scanned it and began pouring out more pancakes. He broke eggs with a one-handed artful flourish, shoveled the cooked pancakes onto a plate, handed them to Tallulah and grinned.

Tallulah tried to close her mouth and stop her stare at the one thing that could sink a woman's heart faster than an orphan-pup look—that was a boyish, carefree grin on a man who hadn't smiled in two centuries.

"Okay," she said glumly, realizing her ship had sailed without her, the hot air had gone out of her balloon and Wyatt had her for the moment.

Then Wyatt flipped the sizzling sausage patty into the trash and said firmly, "No pork."

While Tallulah was busy chewing on this latest turn and on keeping Wyatt away from Fallon, he bent and kissed her lips gently. "Café in Vermont," he explained. "Learned from the best cook anywhere. Jacob was a fiend about maple syrup and breakfasts. No bacon or sausage patties or links or pork chops today, Tallulah."

"They'll mutiny," she grumbled, even as she pictured Leroy. "I'll lose my business."

"Leave the cooking to me," Wyatt said as he patted her shoulder and gently shoved her out the kitchen's swinging doors.

There was nothing more annoying than failing at trying to prove that a man couldn't handle what he had bitten off, Tallulah decided at noon. On the busiest day of the week, Wyatt was thriving in his new role, slinging hash with the best of them, ladling gravy over hot beef sandwiches and serving fettuccine with the steamed vegetarian plate. Customers commented on the artsy touches of parsley and chopped chives that Wyatt had added. When a busload of teenagers stopped for burgers and fries, Wyatt was at his best, plopping thirty burgers across the grill and not failing to remember how many were cheese topped and how many weren't. He was a master at deluxe hamburgers, with onions and without, with "hold the mayo" buns—and with sides of french fries and mushrooms.

Several of the regulars changed their usual orders to Wyatt's double-decker cheeseburgers. Hank Brown heard about the new cook and brought local spit and whittlers, Elmer and Joe, to test the new burgers, dashed with an ultimate, secret spice. By the time Sam, the evening cook, arrived at three o'clock that afternoon, Wyatt had started a new batch of rolls for the supper crowd and had the chicken and tuna salads ready to stuff in the tomatoes.

"Well, okay," Tallulah said reluctantly when she offered to pay him and he refused. "I'll give you lessons to bring you up to par, but you watch it with Fallon."

"Agreed. I'll talk to your dad as soon as possible," he said, bending to check the huge roast for the evening customers and the next day's barbecued sandwiches. "But Fallon asked if I needed a lift home and it would be rude to refuse—"

"Fallon is picking up Miracle from the baby-sitter. You're coming to my volleyball practice, Wyatt. Where I can keep an eye on you. We'll work on your lessons and you can start

Dad's franchise. Tomorrow morning you turn up for lesson number one in meringue.''

"Okay," he said too easily, and Tallulah bent down to see if he was smiling. Wyatt stood and blinked once innocently before he began notching the red radishes into tiny roses.

Tallulah glanced at the lush roses on the counter by the cash register and experienced a sinking feeling.

Watching Tallulah—a hot, sweaty, happy, enthusiastic woman with long legs and curves—bounce around on a gym floor with a collection of her old boyfriends darkened Wyatt's victory. His fingers gripped the gym's bleachers when she playfully swatted one of them on the bottom and the guy returned the favor.

The girlfriends and wives and children of assorted ages cheered on the athletes, while eyeing the newcomer in their midst. Several big-eyed children came to stand in front of Wyatt, staring curiously at him. He patted the bleacher beside him and two boys hopped up and grinned as they sat by him.

When their mothers came to collect their offspring, Wyatt said he'd enjoyed the children. If he could have had his way, he would have had a truckload of children. "Are you Tallulah's new beau?" one of the mothers asked brightly.

"Trying," he returned honestly, watching Tallulah's sweaty T-shirt cling to her breasts and her shorts flap around her bottom. He swallowed when the muscles on her legs flexed in feminine grace as she spiked a ball over the net.

"Belva, our florist, said you bought her only rose bouquet and strolled straight to Tallulah with it. Tallulah is hard to catch. Other men have tried and she fixed them up with wives and girlfriends."

Another woman wiped sticky candy from her girl's mouth and said, "She's skitterish. A bad marriage does that to a woman."

Or a man, Wyatt thought, and wondered about Tallulah's marriage.

When Tallulah reached high to serve, her long, lean body poised to hit the volleyball, Wyatt's heart stopped.

She was more beautiful than a six-pound fighting rainbow trout.

"What did you mean by staring at me that way?" she demanded later as they walked out of the gym to her pickup. "People will get ideas," she stated indignantly, moving in a long-legged easy stride and tossing her athletic bag in the bed of the pickup.

"Just trying to get a head start on my lessons," Wyatt answered darkly as she waved to an ex-boyfriend, then slid into the cab.

When Wyatt sat beside her, Tallulah revved the engine and her pickup soared toward his camper. "I have to be honest with you, Wyatt. There's not a woman in town who suits you. You could be taking these matchmaking lessons without a payoff. Of course, you'll probably be moving on, so maybe you could use your new techniques somewhere else—"

"Tell me about your ex-husband," Wyatt said quietly as he smoothed the damp back of her neck.

Tallulah's big lenses flashed under the street lamp as she looked at him, her fingers tightening on the steering wheel. "No. Now, the first thing you have to learn about being prime material, Remington, is that you can't spring questions like that on a woman. You have to wait until she's ready to tell you about her past, about her ex-loves. By the way, thank you for helping out today. You're very good," she added reluctantly as they skidded to a stop in front of his camper and Wyatt unlatched his free hand from the dashboard.

From his pen, Leroy began squealing his welcome.

"I'm anxious to get started on this romance thing," Wyatt said softly, and wanted to kiss her again. Had he imagined all that hunger, that sense of coming home, when they had kissed before? He ran his finger down her arm and she shivered; Wyatt eased his fingers around her wrist and found it narrow and strong, her pulse racing. He lifted her hand to his lips and kissed the center of it, then he placed it on his shoulder. *He needed her to touch him, having realized suddenly how cold he had been for years.* "How am I doing?"

He had his answer when Tallulah scrambled out of the truck, went to Leroy's pen and began talking with the pig about his day's activities. Wyatt came to stand beside her and slid his hands in his back pockets to keep them from reaching out and tugging her against him. He wanted to rock her in his arms, to ease whatever fears had caused her to bolt away from him.

"The hand-kissing part comes after she encourages you, Wyatt," Tallulah stated flatly. "We haven't even talked about hand holding, and that comes before hand kissing."

"Ah!" he said in an awakening tone that bowed to her wisdom.

Then he bent to kiss her in the moonlight, to warm his lips on hers. He drew her arms gently around his waist as he gathered her closer and rocked her against him. A tiny shudder slid through her and Wyatt cupped her face against his throat. "Your glasses are cold," he whispered against her cheek, then he eased them away from her. He tucked them in his pocket, and when she resisted his arms drawing her to him again, he kissed her so sweetly he thought his heart had flown away. He tasted the corners of her lips and she shuddered, which pleased him.

"This won't do," Tallulah said shakily as she stepped back from him.

Wyatt noted the genuine fear flicking through her eyes, which caught the silvery moon. He threaded his fingers through her soft hair and lifted it to the moonlight, studying the gleaming tips and absorbing the fragrance.

"I want you," he said quietly, and knew that lovemaking with Tallulah would shatter him forever.

She looked horrified, her eyes widening. She jerked her glasses from his pocket, jammed them on her nose and peered up at him. "Wyatt, you are truly hopeless. Getting to this stage is much farther down the romantic line."

"Cutting to the chase seems honorable enough if the woman sees the man coming," he offered huskily. "It seems sporting."

"Huh," she said disbelievingly, flicking away a strand of hair from her cheek in that impatient way of hers. He wondered if she would make love as impatiently, and pushed his smile away as she continued. "You are truly hopeless. Think of it this way—romance has to simmer like a good pot of chili, allowing the flavors to blend. You can't dish up a statement like wanting a woman until the moment is ripe, when the chili pepper and the onions mate."

"Oh," he returned huskily, looking slowly down her body and wanting her with every particle of his heart and soul. "Mate," he repeated slowly, and thought about the experience with Tallulah.

She peered up at him, then reached to test his forehead with her hand. "You're a bit warm, Wyatt. I hope you're not catching Norm's whatever."

"My heart seems to be racing a little fast," he whispered as Tallulah's breasts nudged him gently. She looked up at him worriedly and lightly eased her hand down to his heart. His fingers closed around her wrist to keep her palm there over the heavy, rapid beat.

Who was this woman who cared so much for others? Who tended the old and the sick and the worried with her heart? Who protected Fallon and Miracle as fiercely as though they were her own family? Who didn't think of herself as truly desirable?

"What did he do to you?" Wyatt asked softly, his fears for her leaping like tiny, venomous snakes.

Four

"He's nice, but he seems so lonely," Fallon said the next afternoon when she came to pick up her paycheck, bringing Miracle with her. June hovered near Elegance as Fallon looked at Wyatt through the café's windows while he stood on the sidewalk, surrounded by men with new W.R. fly lures stuck in their ball caps.

"I want you."

Tallulah shook her head, trying to clear it of Wyatt's voice and her sleepless night.

No man had ever told her he wanted her in that quiet, husky tone, too rich and too aching to be false. He'd frightened her so badly that she'd run to her pickup and roared to safety. She'd skidded to a stop in front of her house, raced through her picket-fence gate, over the steps and through the heavy door, bolting it behind her. Panting with the fear ripping through her, she'd sped up the stairs to her bedroom and dived into bed, pulling the heavy ruffled quilt up to her chin. She'd stared at the moon through her ruffled lace curtains and trembled.

Tallulah Jane Ames, a woman who would fight for a cause or a wounded soul, no matter what the risk was to herself, had sat there fully dressed under a quilt, trembling with fear and staring at the moon as if she expected a caped vampire to glide down on a moonbeam and...

"I want you."

Wyatt had stirred fears that she had locked away for years, and now they pursued her with vengeance—when she wasn't remembering his sweet kiss or how he had rocked her gently in his arms. It was his champion orphan-pup look, she'd decided around two o'clock. Wyatt could display a first-class battered, lonely-soul look. Without being aware, she must have taken it, hook, line and sinker.

She cursed him for opening the yawning dark void.

Tallulah had long ago stopped thinking of herself as a desirable woman. She'd been safe until Wyatt started casting sweet kisses and hungry looks her way.

She never wanted that pain again....

Her eyes hurt from tears she didn't want to release as she damned Wyatt Remington from the depths of her broken heart.

For years she'd tended Elegance and everyone in it and had placed her emotions as a woman on the highest, hardest-to-reach shelf. Until her marriage to Jack, she'd lived with her father and taken care of him. Now she had her own home, but she still saw to her father's needs with the help of Lottie, his housekeeper.

"I want you."

That morning, Wyatt had again taken Norm's place behind the breakfast grill as if he'd worked there for years. When Norm had returned at noon, feeling better and ready to finish his shift, Wyatt had nodded to Tallulah, who was keeping her distance from him. Then he'd had left the café carrying a sack of goodies for Leroy.

Now he was standing on the street just as she was about to leave her shift. From the motions of the men's hands, they were discussing fly casting. Tallulah made a mental note to add a "You clean your catch—we'll cook it" to the Tall Order's menu. June would be a flurry of fishing with Mr. W. R. Lures in the neighborhood....

"I like him," Fallon was saying as she straightened Miracle's new hair bow. "I hope he finds what he's looking for. He needs some happiness. Everyone does."

"Fallon..." Tallulah began, uncertain how to present Wyatt's unsuitability as matchmaking potential to the young woman.

Wyatt entered the café just as Tom Freeman slipped a quarter in the jukebox; a slow-dancing song swirled through the café and Maizie and Joe Brown, an elderly couple very much in love, stood up to dance like young lovebirds.

Wyatt's gaze locked with Tallulah's immediately. The simmering hunger she'd seen in his eyes in last night's moonlight warmed, taking her breath.

Then Miracle was tugging at his faded jeans, raising her arms to him and grinning. "Danth," she lisped.

Wyatt's expression shifted, and immediately the flickering desire was replaced by a tender, aching look. With deliberate care, he bent to Miracle and gathered her gently up into his arms until he stood straight.

"Danth," Miracle said again, placing her chubby hands on his cheeks and testing the afternoon stubble there.

"Look at that. He's so sweet," Fallon was saying wistfully, wrapping her arms around herself as if hugging dreams tightly against her.

Tallulah glanced at Fallon, saw the hunger and the ache written on her young face beneath the mop of curls she always wore as if shielding a bit of herself from the world.

When Wyatt began to dance slowly with Miracle, her round face beaming, Tallulah swallowed sharply and realized that tears burned at her lids.

Fallon sighed wistfully and clasped her hands to her chest. "I never knew my own father," she whispered shakily. "But Mom told me about him. He wasn't nice. Not like Wyatt. I've always wanted Miracle to have the father I didn't have . . . one like Wyatt. Every time I look at him, my heart feels weird. Probably because in my life there haven't been that many nice men."

Tallulah swallowed hard. She watched Wyatt talk gently to Miracle as they moved around the floor. His long, lean, T-shirt-and-worn-jeans, all-male look was softened by the little girl's pink-striped, ruffled sunsuit. He was absorbed in the girl and she was fascinated with him, touching his face and smiling shyly. He closed his eyes when he nuzzled her dark curls, and his frown said he was deeply moved by the child's sweetness.

"Isn't that a sight to make a body cry?" Norm said behind Tallulah. He sniffed and wiped a tear from his eye with a corner of his apron. "Onions," he explained unevenly.

When the dance was over and Wyatt gently, slowly, lowered Miracle to the floor, Fallon sighed wistfully. When Miracle reached to hug him and kiss him, his eyes widened as though he was stunned. An emotion shifted over his hard face as if part of his soul had touched heaven.

Norm sobbed aloud as Wyatt watched Miracle run to Fallon.

"Thank you," she said quietly, and skirted by him to the door.

Wyatt watched Fallon hurry past the café's outside windows, and when he turned back to Tallulah, pain flickered through his black eyes and lined his face.

"Kids get to a guy, don't they?" Norm said knowingly, and asked Wyatt to come back and check the excellent new batch of steaks.

But Wyatt was standing in front of Tallulah, looking down at her, searching the very depths of her soul in that quiet intent way of his.

He frightened her. She tried to breathe, and found Wyatt's large hand drawing hers up to his lips. Over their hands, he gazed at her with questions she didn't want to think about, much less answer. "Fallon isn't for you," she whispered shakily after she cleared her throat.

"What about you, Tallulah Jane?" he murmured against her palm. She kept those words locked tight in her hand when she tore it away.

"No," she said softly, and whizzed away to make cherry milk shakes for the Browns.

Wyatt watched her offer a second piece of pie to Mack Jones, then he turned abruptly. When she passed him, he said quietly, "I'm walking you home. You can give me a lesson on the way."

Then he headed out the door, and was soon surrounded by the ball-cap crowd. Their caps were studded with his lures, resembling an Easter-hat brigade.

After a week of Wyatt's invasion of the Tall Order's kitchen, Norm had adjusted to sharing his grill during the café's busy hours. He laughed as he swapped tall cooking stories with Wyatt. Norm began to use air freshener around the café and watched curiously as Tallulah made batter-fried onions every day.

Tallulah hadn't adjusted to anything. Her life was undone, the safety whisked away each time Wyatt came near her.

Dancing with her ex-boyfriends to jukebox music only served to distress her; she realized that Wyatt could unbalance her as no man had done since Jack. She'd lost hours of sleep and even onion-ring therapy didn't work.

She dreamed about his deep, husky voice whispering, "I want you."

The first time Wyatt followed her directions for shaping pie crust, she almost melted as his big hands lovingly worked the dough. His fingers shaped each point of the crust in the same methodical way he had plucked the wings of his lures. Her body was constantly on the alert, tensed and overreacting.

Tallulah was pleased with Wyatt's progress concerning Fallon. He acted friendly, but not flirtatious. Tallulah could not deny him Miracle's wish to dance to the jukebox music; her heart ached when she saw Wyatt swallow shakily and gently lift the girl into his arms. He danced with her as though the moment was the most beautiful, the most treasured in his life; each time they danced, Tallulah's heart tightened. Tears, which weren't caused by onions, came to her eyes.

Every afternoon when she was finished with her shift, Wyatt collected her for their exchange of lessons.

Tallulah had decided she might need a little help with her casts. Michaelson's Sporting Goods store shouldn't reap all the rewards of her giving lessons to Mr. W. R. Lures. He was grim, but patient, as she cast into the stream, losing several of his choice lures. In return, she explained how a woman acted if she was interested, and that perhaps if he would stop scowling, as he did when she cast, he might be more acceptable.

Wyatt seemed to note quite carefully the distance she managed to keep from him. Her stomach fluttered if he came too near and she edged away from him. When Wyatt entered the café, she could serve twice as many orders and Norm complained about cook slavery, so she switched to polishing all the stainless steel in sight.

The dark amusement in Wyatt's eyes wasn't shared by Tallulah.

The second week of June, the butcher complained when Tallulah canceled her pork orders—she'd become very sensitive to Leroy's beady eyes. The butcher flatly told her he believed all vegetarians would go to a fiery, evil place in the afterlife. He added that it mystified him why everyone wanted to walk Wyatt's porker up and down Main Street and that the added interest in local fishing was killing his profit.

Her father was delirious with success on the day of Wyatt's casting debut in Elegance and had wistfully asked his only daughter to attend. The Saturday event drew horseshoe tossers and the garden club's annual plant sale. Leroy was to lead the children's pig parade and little oinkers were tied near shady spots and squealing for attention.

Tallulah hadn't asked to be the volunteer for Wyatt's casting demonstration. She hadn't asked for him to stand closely behind her and to place his left hand over hers, manipulating the line. Her right hand, guided by his, went back and cast forward into the colored rings floating on the shallow artificial pond beside Michaelson's Sporting Goods store.

No one in Elegance could miss Mr. W. R. Lures bending to nibble on her earlobe while he whispered shocking things he wanted to do to her—like spread her over him and taste the sweat between her breasts after she finished playing volleyball.

With her backside locked to Wyatt's hard body, she could not miss his need. Or her own, as her legs went weak.

Or the delighted grin of her father as he watched with approval. No doubt he was thinking of getting free advertising in the W.R. Lures Catalog....

Miracle was delighted as Wyatt cuddled her in one arm and cast into the colored ring of her choice. She was enchanted when he placed Leroy's leash in her hand for the children's parade.

Tallulah had found her hand encased in his as Miracle pranced Leroy down the street. The little girl stopped several times to proudly fuss with the porker's flower-decked straw hat. When Wyatt walked her home after the festivities, he noted a loose hinge on her screen door and tightened it with his knife. Tallulah hemmed a bit, anxious to get away, and then Wyatt drew her slowly against him and kissed her until she melted.

Or did she melt because of the things he was telling her? How he wanted her.... She suddenly discovered she was arching against him, laminating her body to his and kissing him with heat that she must have hoarded since her teenage years. She exploded in volcanic needs when Wyatt gently tempted her tongue into his mouth and suckled it rhythmically. When his large hands trailed up to her ribs, she ached to have them over her breasts. With a hungry groan, Wyatt slowly, tenderly closed his hands over her breasts.

He inhaled and sighed appreciatively, caressing her shape until she felt more than adequate as a desirable woman—

There in the June evening, sheltered by the vines concealing her front porch, Tallulah had experienced her first session of sitting on a loving man's lap as Wyatt settled into the huge wooden armchair on her porch and gathered her close, fitting his chin over her head and stroking her gently until she stopped trembling. Then he said, "Tallulah," in a soft Southern drawl that frightened her so badly that she ripped herself away and ran inside the house.

The next Sunday afternoon—the third week of June— Wyatt lay on the bank behind her, wearing only his jeans and looking very edible, while she tried to concentrate on her casting and keep her cattail quota very low. The late-afternoon sun spread across his dark skin like golden butter, and Tallulah peeked slyly for the single gray hair that haunted her dreams. He'd opened his jeans' waistband after the picnic lunch they'd eaten and the image of his tall body on the worn patchwork quilt was distracting.

"You've got to give a woman room before you move in for the kill," Tallulah said absently, focusing on the trout rising to the top of the water. They stayed away from any area she cast into.

"You can't look all hot and sultry when women are at odd moments, like when you were staring at me after the volleyball game. And there was no reason for you to tell Johnny that the 'butt-patting' days with me were over. You looked hostile when you said it."

"You were sweaty," he noted as he sucked a stalk of grass and watched her cast. "And I *was* hostile. Don't snap your forearm forward so soon."

"Rear patting is standard in the athletic business, Wyatt. Watch more football on television.... So what if I sweat? Women sweat, too, you know. I played a hard game." She was too tense, realizing that Wyatt's dark gaze hadn't moved from her. She wiped her sweaty palm on her cutoff denim shorts and began to cast again. "You shouldn't ever, ever tell a woman that she sweats, Wyatt. Bad form."

"Come here," he murmured so quietly that the stream's ripple almost covered the words.

The shaking aspens shivered in the slight, fragrant breeze, and birds called.

Tallulah stopped in midcast. Whatever had been simmering inside her since she'd seen Wyatt bang his hammer against her loose shutter at the crack of dawn began to heat.

"Come here, Tallulah," he repeated in that soft Southern drawl that caused her to tremble.

She swallowed, remembering Wyatt's expression as he listened to her hot and nasty "lunatics not sleeping in on a Sunday morning" speech. He'd looked at the overlong T-shirt covering her, then down her bare legs very slowly. He'd wrapped her close to him and whispered huskily, "Take your choice. Let's make love right here on your back porch, or let's go fishing."

She'd managed to waylay the fishing trip by puttering around the Tall Order Café and talking with people while she packed a picnic lunch. Then Wyatt had strolled in, nodded at her father, who was drooling over a W.R. Lures Catalog, and announced he was taking Tallulah fishing. She noted that he was freshly shaved, which accounted for his short absence from the café. Within minutes, she was tucked against him in his pickup truck and Leroy was stashed at Miracle and Fallon's home.

He lay on the bank now. The waiting was over; her time had come. She could take Wyatt's delicious lure or she could face her fears for an eternity.

"Why?" she asked carefully as she braced the fishing rod against a limb.

"Come into my office," he said, patting the quilt beside him.

She gazed down at him and knew she wanted Wyatt Remington more than she wanted the June air filled with mountain scents and sunshine.

More than she wanted the biggest fighting trout in the stream.

Wyatt locked his fingers around her ankle and returned her look, only his was as dark and sultry as a hot summer storm in the South with lightning cracking on the horizon. "You come here," he whispered huskily, caressing her skin and letting her know that she could choose the sport and the pace.

Or she could walk away.

She tilted her head to one side, not willing to let him have it all his own way. "The man-ordering-woman bit is out of mode, Wyatt Remington," she whispered back unevenly.

"Come down here and tell me about it," he said with a cocky, boyish grin that set her heart racing. "I want to know more. I think I'm improving. Maybe Gothic guys can learn after all."

"And don't leer," she added, allowing him to tug her down to the quilt. His touch was light, so light, guiding her down, that she knew she could ease away in a heartbeat and stand free and alone....

He smiled in a way that fascinated her, then rolled to his side, looking down at her. "I appreciate your input," he said softly, running his fingertip around her mouth.

"Don't try what you've learned on Fallon," she warned, and closed her mind against the other women Wyatt might have looked at in that hungry, hot, tense way.

"Not a chance," he agreed between kisses so sweet they took her breath away. His open hand rested on her stomach now, beneath her T-shirt, caressing her skin, until his fingers slid under her waistband and spanned her abdomen.

She couldn't breathe and didn't want to; breathing might take away the sweet expectancy. She couldn't draw her eyes away from Wyatt's until he looked down to where her fingers had locked on his wrist. "The last time I made love with a woman was years ago," he whispered in a deep, dark voice filled with slow, Southern nights and sweet magnolias. "It's been a long time.... I'm monogamous, I guess."

"Monogamous is good," she heard herself say breathlessly as his fingers massaged her stomach a little lower and her waistband popped open. "I'm that way myself."

"Could be that a man gets out of practice."

His rich voice poured through the June sunshine as she watched him study her bare legs.

"Could be," she agreed with the last atom of air in her lungs, closing her eyes as his fingers curved intimately over her.

Tallulah's body tightened and her inner muscles contracted in gentle rhythm; she was drawn to the very peak of passion to twist and quiver for a heartbeat or an eternity. Like a dove escaping into the blue sky, a cry soared out of her, high and aching, and she was certain that it frightened the trout at the very bottom of the stream.

Forcing her lids open, she found Wyatt frowning down at her, his expression guarded. "Don't you laugh," she muttered, taking refuge in the nearest solid thing—Wyatt's long, safe body. She buried her hot face against his throat and shivered while he cuddled her against him and talked to her softly.

"And now, Tallulah, you're going to tell me about Jack... about what he did to hurt you." Wyatt stroked her back and added, "And tell me why each time you see a baby you look like you've been to hell and back."

Her fingertips dug into Wyatt's sun-warmed shoulders and she struggled with the fear and balanced it against the safety he offered. She eased away from him and lay looking up at the pine needles glimmering in the sunlight overhead. Wyatt gave her the space she needed to think, to come to terms with a secret she had admitted to no one else.

She'd run too long and too fast, and now the darkness yawned before her. She swallowed and lay thinking, rummaging through the years until she found the words. "It was mental abuse. I know that now. I loved Jack, and a marriage without children would have been perfect. Or we could have adopted them. But he thought being a man consisted of making a child, preferably a boy. When children didn't come, he began making small, hurtful remarks about me not being woman enough. I offered to have tests and Jack didn't want them.... I guess maybe he didn't want to know."

Wyatt kissed her forehead and rocked her against him gently. She lay close to him, feeling very safe. "Because I loved him so much, I took the blame without questioning him. He decided I was 'barren' and maybe I am. I guess I came to think the way he did... that a barren woman isn't desirable, isn't really a woman."

She tried for a smile, which failed as she met Wyatt's gaze. Her lips trembled and she realized tears had been trailing down her cheeks. She dashed them away and tried again for a brave smile, which wobbled and died. "Silly, isn't it? It still hurts after all these years. In the end, I didn't want to know if I could bear children. I just didn't want to know, because if I couldn't, Jack would be right— In the end, I didn't excite him at all. He didn't want me.... I know the reality of all this, or nonreality. But it still comes back.''

Wyatt's curse about what he'd like to do to her ex-husband was dark and flat and concerned. His fingers shook as he soothed her tears and drew her face to his, kissing her lids, her nose, her mouth. "You're a woman, Tallulah Jane, filled with heart and love," he whispered shakily, kissing her trembling lips. "Any man, except a certified idiot, would be proud to have you in his life.''

She tried to lighten the moment, hovering there on the edge of her pain, amazed that she had just shared it with Wyatt. "Do all Gothic guys kiss a lot?" she asked in a wobbly tone.

Wyatt ignored the question; he was too busy kissing her. When she caught her breath, she realized her fingers were gripping his hair, keeping his mouth on hers. "We're going to do this, aren't we, Wyatt?"

"Sure are, Tallulah Jane. We're going to make love and burn out any doubts about you not being desirable, because if I don't have you soon, I'll embarrass myself... that's how undesirable you are.''

She laughed out loud, feeling suddenly gay and young and very attractive as Wyatt shakily removed her clothing. He kissed each new inch he uncovered and teased the tips of her breasts into two aching points. His mouth over them, suckling and nibbling, didn't help the ache a bit. In fact, the ache grew to fill her whole body. Nothing helped until he settled over her without a stitch of clothing between them.

He looked down at her, his grin almost shy and very tender. She eased away a wave of hair that crossed his forehead and smoothed the lines between his brows. Wyatt nestled his length along her body gently, as if he were coming home and meant to stay.

"Take it easy with me, Tallulah Jane. I'm an old man, and there haven't been any surveys that I know of to see if

Gothic guys can survive lovemaking the way I want to make love to you.''

Tallulah smiled slowly and ran her bare sole along Wyatt's bulky calf. She measured the mercy in her heart for Wyatt Remington and decided he was on his own.

"Come here," she whispered, stroking his trembling shoulders. "I'll take care of you, Mr. W. R. Lures."

Wyatt's expression as he eased into her was as though he was experiencing the most beautiful event of his life. Tallulah remembered how he had looked when he danced with Miracle, and thought what a wonderful father he would have made. She held her breath and said softly, "You're shivering. Are you cold?"

"Not likely," he muttered against her throat. "I'm concentrating."

"On what?" she asked with a grin, as he cupped her bottom and locked them together.

"Weren't you the one who said I couldn't concentrate and talk at the same time?" he asked in a tone husky with passion and laced with humor. "Any true sportsman knows that fit is important. That's what I'm concentrating on," he managed unevenly.

"I'll help," she promised, before her body began tightening around his.

"Mercy" was all he said before they sailed off into the June sunset on a hot, tight voyage that burst somewhere near the sun.

Wyatt refused to let Tallulah go, drawing her closer to him and easing the quilt over them as they watched the late-afternoon sun flicker through the leaves overhead. With a sigh, she settled closer to him and nestled her nose in the hair on his chest. "You have a gray hair here," she noted.

"I've aged in the past few minutes or so," he explained with a long, slow sigh of pleasure.

But she was really thinking about what Wyatt had said at the very height of their passion, just as her cry escaped her soul and as he gave himself to her in the most beautiful way.... *"I love you, Tallulah.... Love you...."*

She squeezed her eyes closed. Though she hadn't experienced it before now, she'd heard that passion could wring a statement like that from a man.

"I love you, Tallulah Jane," Wyatt said sleepily over her head. "Get used to it," he ordered with a huge yawn. "I haven't slept for weeks and it's your fault," he continued in that same, sleepy-soft, sexy Southern voice.

Tallulah's eyes widened, fear quivering around her, chilling her more than the approaching cool Montana night. She scrambled to her feet and began pulling on her clothing.

Wyatt frowned up at her. "What are you doing?"

"I love you, Tallulah...." She hadn't thought of love, of the pain it could bring, the tearing away of her soul, leaving her ripped and... She hopped on one foot, the tiny stones hurting her sole as she jammed on one jogger, then the other.

She'd gotten her left shoe on her right foot and vice versa, and her T-shirt on backward.

"Get back in this bed," Wyatt commanded in the tone of a husband who said that very thing to his wife every night.

"Do you know how old we are?" she asked him as she frantically tried to stuff her panties and bra into the pockets of her cutoff shorts.

Wyatt ran his fingers through his hair and she blushed when she saw that he was aroused again. "Cover yourself," she managed shakily.

"I love you...." She wasn't ready for a man invading her life, making her feel desirable and ordering her back to bed with the irate tone of a husband.

Wyatt didn't look like a husband, bored and wanting to snore.

He trailed his eyes up her legs and to the tight nubs of her breasts as though he wanted a second helping. "I think I'm getting the hang of this matchmaking-lesson thing," he purred. "Why don't you come down here and tell me more," he invited, his dark gaze smoldering in the half light of the filtered sunset.

"Oh," she said airily as she glanced anywhere but down at him, "I think we'd better be going along, don't you? Have to get up early and bake those pies, you know. Monday is a busy day at the café."

"Leroy is staying with Miracle and Fallon tonight," he insisted hopefully.

"I'm certain he'll enjoy himself," she said firmly, and turned her back while he dressed.

"I'll be lonely," Wyatt stated as he came to stand behind her and buried his warm face against her throat. He rocked her close to him and whispered, "Don't be frightened, Tallulah. This is all new to me, too."

While she shivered, despite being locked in his heat, Wyatt murmured against her skin, "Next time we'll take it slow. You got me rattled.... Lovemaking with an impatient, red-haired whirlwind can off-balance a man's style. Especially when he's out of practice. Practice does improve skill, you know."

Then he leaned close to her ear and said firmly, "Now, get this straight, Tallulah Jane. You are not passing me off like one of the backup boys, playing matchmaker, when I come too close. 'Cause I'm already close, and I'm staying that way. And the only woman I'm leching after is you...."

He laughed outright when she twisted free and scrambled up the bank. She stopped at the top while Wyatt whistled; she wondered when the last time was that she'd heard a Gothic guy laugh.

She huddled in the corner of the pickup as Wyatt slid into the driver's seat. She clasped her hands and studied them as they trembled.

Wyatt looked at her from beneath his lashes and said quietly, "Get over here. I need to practice shifting and placing my hand on my best girl's knee."

"Wyatt," she said as she scooted over next to him and allowed him to place her hand on his thigh. "What will people say? When you take me fishing and we never catch anything and you being a master angler? They'll know.... Do you remember just how old we are?"

"Shoot. We're just kids, Tallulah. Feels like it, anyway," he added with a grin and a sweet kiss.

Five

Wyatt began testing his new lure at dawn. The Tallulah, a whimsical, glistening, fire-red-and-sexy-black affair, rode the stream in a high, proud fashion, zigging quickly along on the top of the water like her sleek namesake. Designing and making this Tallulah was as close as Wyatt knew he'd better come to the real one last night—because if ever a woman was frightened, it was Tallulah.

She needed time to think, to weigh what had happened between them.

Wyatt glanced at the shadowy nook where they had made love and sighed deeply. The third Sunday in June was a date he would never forget. His need for Tallulah had risen so strongly during the night that he'd almost placed aside his design and his notes and climbed the sturdy trellis to her bedroom window.

He flipped the Tallulah out on the dark stream, played her this way and that and avoided the trout running after her like that pack of fanny-patting ex-boyfriends. She skittered on the water, the dawn catching the dew on her feathered wings, and Wyatt jerked the line to avoid a five-pound trout attacking her.

He'd intended to lie beside her and tell her about Fallon and Miracle—his other loves—and the family he had back in Georgia, who had worried with him all these years.

Wyatt gritted his teeth and snapped the line away from another pink-sided iridescent poacher.

Before he'd buried himself inside Tallulah's warmth, he'd wanted to gently tell her that he was in love with her and to tell her about his life—how he'd roamed the world hunting his daughter and how he'd arranged for his daughter and granddaughter's safety away from the city streets. He'd wanted to tell how her how his emotions ran deep and true and that if she'd allow him to love her, it would be the sweetest event in his life. He wanted to spread his life in front of her and tell her how much he admired her loving ways...except with the ex-boyfriends.

From the way she acted, from the tightness of her body, Wyatt decided the ex-boyfriends hadn't gotten as close as he had, and they weren't going to in the future, either. Monogamous was how he and Tallulah were going to stay—

He jerked the line a bit too quickly as a silvery streak surfaced near the ripples and followed the Tallulah past the cattails.

Wyatt scowled at three trout following the lure and cast it out of their reach—they reminded him of the ex-boyfriends.

He loved her. Wyatt had mated for his lifetime. Tallulah was the other part of him and he was made whole just by looking at her. For a man who'd loved once, or rather mistaken sex for love when he was in his early twenties, Wyatt was as certain as when a fighting fish took his lure and ran with it.

With that love came fears that chilled him to his bones—what did he know about loving? The face-to-face kind, the everyday kind, with a woman who had needs of her own?

The mysteries of feminine logic terrified him. A man could sink in the tiny, emotional quirks women sometimes hoarded.

Thanks to Tallulah's ex-husband, she was wary of anything resembling a permanent hook.

Wyatt cast again, frowning at the frothing, peaceful stream. What he didn't know he'd learn, and he'd try again.

He snorted as the dawn slid through the pines and caught the glittering red-bug lure. Tallulah was very fast—the woman and the lure. Tallulah—the woman—had taken him before he was ready, before he'd told her who he was and why he looked at Fallon that way.

A trout surged out of the water, mouth open and ready for Tallulah— Wyatt's body gave a hard sensual jerk, just as he skillfully tugged the lure away.

Wyatt shivered, needing the morning chill against his skin. The morning after giving his heart, he would have preferred to be holding his ladylove and feasting on their love. The dawn was like the morning after his wedding without his bride.

But fear had flashed in the silvery, teary depths of her eyes and he knew he would wait.

Actually, Wyatt admitted to feeling very fragile. She'd taken him too fast, and the protection he'd stashed in his wallet had stayed there. He was a failure at the Romeo business; maybe he was out of step as a lover.

He hadn't meant to spring his love on her so soon; she'd been hurt and was wary, which explained everything. Tallulah had a right to her fears, to search them out and to discover that he wouldn't hurt her....

The thought chafed until he recalled their lovemaking, then he grinned and enjoyed rescuing the Tallulah lure from the hungry brown trout racing after her. After all, Tallulah had pitted herself against him. She had locked him to her and had kissed him and ruined his patience. She'd cried out, the high, soulful, keening sound sailing around him as he gave himself to her, so deeply and so truly as if they had loved before.

Then there was the soft flutter of her heart against him, as though she'd just run her race to him ... and later, when her muscles had stopped quivering and she'd melted against him, her sigh was as sweet as the mourning dove cooing in the sumacs near him.

Wyatt frowned over his shoulder to the place where they had lain; he would have to move more cautiously, to keep the pressure up, keep the line taut. Tallulah needed time to know him and the love that would deepen for her each day.

He intended to stay near for the rest of his life ... and to love her so well that the damage her ex-husband had done would be erased.... Above the coo of the mourning dove, Wyatt heard his short, flat curse for the man who had hurt Tallulah.

Tallulah missed the sugar shaker and watched the mound of spilled sugar grow on the counter as she thought about Wyatt's lovemaking.

The pyramid of sugar glistened in the morning sun shafting through the café window. She stroked it with her fingertip.

When compared with Jack's—the only man she had given her body to—Wyatt's lovemaking seemed from another galaxy. She sighed, fighting the lack of sleep and the strange, warm, fuzzy, drained tingle lodged deep in her body.

As fit as she was, in shape from every sport that kept her busy and sleeping at night, lovemaking with Wyatt had alerted her to a deeper restlessness. She'd awakened in a tangle of sheets, her body throbbing and her heart filling with joy—

I love you....

The kiss at her doorstep was enough to sizzle an egg on a December snowbank. Wyatt had gathered her to him, nuzzled her throat until she melted and had grinned into the damp curve of her neck. "You smell like us," he'd said huskily, sliding his hand under her braless T-shirt to gently caress her breast. "That's good."

She'd been shocked; Jack's disdain had flashed through her mind, then slid away as Wyatt had gathered her closer.

While he rocked her slowly, he began to tell her about how she tasted, and how her body fitted him like a glove, and how he felt when he gave himself to her—as if they were one soul, one heart. There was more to how he felt than sharing their bodies, he'd whispered. There was the emotion that would never change, that would keep him close to her when they were rocking side by side in their sunset years.

She found herself clinging to him, standing on tiptoe in her mismatched shoes and looking up into his dark, hungry eyes. "Don't you say you love me, Wyatt Remington," she'd ordered shakily. "We're too old to say things we don't mean—"

"Do," he'd returned simply, kissing her nose.

"Do not."

"It's true," he'd whispered unevenly.

"No."

"Sure is, Tallulah Jane. Deep and true. You've caught me. You showed no mercy and you landed me...scooped me into your net." Then he'd kissed her one more time and patted her bottom and groaned hungrily before he'd walked away whistling "Dixie."

An hour spent bouncing frantically on her indoor trampoline hadn't settled her nerves. The long, scented bath had caused her to think of the earth scents welling up around them as they'd made love, the dark fragrance that was Wyatt's alone.

Now Norm came to stand at her side, drinking ice water and looking over her shoulder to the spilled sugar. "Wyatt, huh? At least drawing his name in sugar is better than cooking onions every day. I've started having nightmares about being squeezed to death by a giant Idaho Sweet."

Tallulah stared, horrified to find she had written "Wyatt" within the borders of a big sugary heart. She barely had time to scrape it away before Wyatt entered the café with her father, who was waving a W.R. Lures Catalog like a trophy.

Wyatt's dark eyes found her immediately. He nodded to her father, then drew change from his worn jeans and pushed a quarter into the jukebox. When the slow music began, Wyatt walked to Tallulah, who was frantically making a new pot of coffee, and took her hand to draw her out to the floor.

There in the Tall Order Café, during the Monday-morning breakfast rush at eight o'clock, Wyatt gathered her close to him and swayed to the music. "'Morning, Tallulah," he whispered against her ear, his fingers caressing her hand and her back.

"Jitterbugging is my specialty with customers," she suggested as Wyatt swayed with her.

"Times change.... Slow dancing has its benefits," Wyatt returned in his drawl. He tucked her hand close to his heart and looked down at her. "How are you feeling?"

She looked up into his eyes and knew that he wanted her now, knew that he had banked his needs last evening.... "You're a mover," she whispered unevenly.

"You're a fine catch," he said gently. "A real keeper."

"I'm not used to all this," she replied after swallowing.

"I know...that's why I'm picking you up for fishing lessons this afternoon."

"I'm gardening my roses, Wyatt." She couldn't let him plan her life, after all. "Manuring is very important this time of year."

"I'll help. There's a big one out at the stream with your name on him," Wyatt murmured heavily, unevenly, against her ear, and sent tingles running up her spine. "He looks like about six pounds of sheer, mean, fighting fury...of course, if you've decided the fight is too much for you and you'd like a safer sport, I'm ready for that, too...although when I'm next to you, I'm short on warranties and guarantees."

She was having difficulty breathing, so aware was she of his hard length, his hard thighs gently bumping her own as they danced. She sucked air into the top of her lungs and forced it out shakily while she remembered his shoulders catching the sunlight as he'd moved over her.

"Leroy is lonesome for you," Wyatt added softly. "And so am I."

When Jason Kannally went on vacation, Wyatt took his place on Tallulah's team for the playoff on the Fourth of July. Volleyball wasn't his sport; he wasn't that agile and he simmered when Tallulah yelled at him for missing a served ball. She commented on his "you don't have to kill the ball" form while they walked home, and Wyatt found himself kissing her with the hunger he had leashed for days.

This morning, he'd ached from head to toe and could barely demonstrate during his casting hour at Michaelson's. He'd eased onto his usual stool at the Tall Order and watched gloomily while Tallulah had served a second slice of pie to Arnold Riggs, an old boyfriend who was very good at volleyball.

Now, afternoon shimmered in greens and golds as Wyatt stopped casting and concentrated on the woman sharing the stream. Tallulah moved restlessly, tromping up and down the bank in the waders he had loaned her. She cast upstream and downstream, slaying cattails and bushes and once catching the backside of Wyatt's jeans. She'd tipped over a huge box of lures as she'd run toward him, her eyes anxious, and quickly tangled them both in her line. He'd gotten in a few kisses before she'd squirmed away.

Tallulah was impatient, a casting whirlwind, determined to get "the big one." Her reddish blond hair caught the sunset, her long lean body outlined against the dark brush bordering the stream as she cast. Despite her lacking technique, she was the most beautiful vision Wyatt had ever seen, his fishing vest shrouding her, the sun catching her long bare legs above the waders. To him, the sight of Tallulah wearing his clothes was too sweet for words. His muscles protested and he groaned as he raised his pole now, blocking her line from him as it hooked a pine cone and dragged it back into the stream.

Wyatt inhaled and frowned with the aching pain caused by yesterday's volleyball game and by his current need for Tallulah.

"Wyatt?" Tallulah was asking, placing her pole on the rocks and walking to him in the large waders. The sun gleamed on the shifting slender muscles of her thighs. "Are you all right?"

"Hell, no," he said flatly, meaning it and feeling very fragile and wounded. For a man who had been patient and methodical all his life, he found himself tight with impatience.

She stopped in front of him and squinted against the dying sun. "You've been nursing a bad mood since I yelled at you. I'm the captain of the volleyball team, Wyatt. It's my job to yell."

He inhaled, determined to keep his mouth closed until Tallulah put it to better use than arguing.

"Did you really name that lure for me?"

"Uh-huh."

"Why?"

"Watch." Wyatt worked the lure, and the red-and-black affair skittered daintily on top of the stream, riding the water over the ripples and along the bank. Trout lazing in the stream surged toward it, churning the water as Wyatt recast upstream. Tallulah placed her hand on his arm and her fingers tightened. She breathed hard, the vest covering her breast against his arm. When he should have cast again, Wyatt let the lure ride the water downstream just so he could feel her close, the battered vest nudging against his arm.

"Wyatt, I don't know why, but there is something very indecent about that lure.... Do you really think there is a big one with my name on it?" Tallulah said in a distracted tone as she scanned the stream anxiously.

"I know there is. One just for you," he said firmly, as he locked his legs against the sensual tightening running through him.

After taking Leroy on his evening promenade around Elegance, Tallulah had the feeling she was being courted and every male in the town was being warned off as Wyatt placed his hand on the small of her back. When they arrived at her home, Tallulah looked down at the toe of Wyatt's boot, which was successfully blocking her effort to gently close the door.

"Leroy just ran into the house," Wyatt said slowly, his lips slightly swollen from her hungry kiss.

She liked kissing Wyatt. She liked pitting herself against his firm, somewhat grim mouth and coaxing it into a hungry softness. She liked sliding her tongue across his lips and enticing his to play awhile. She loved holding his shoulders, latching herself to him and seeing just what she could stir up. Wyatt was too slow, too methodical, his hands taking forever to glide up to her breasts, there to pluck and smooth and caress.

She hadn't pitted herself against Jack or any of her ex-boyfriends, who were really just in need of keeping until someone suitable came along and claimed them. Tallulah didn't feel like placing Wyatt in her safekeeping for another woman.

She felt like hoarding him away and pitting herself against him....

She couldn't afford to commit herself to another man, to open herself to the pain of rejection—Wyatt's dark, smoldering expression didn't look as if he was getting ready to reject her....

Tallulah sensed that her yelling at Wyatt had touched something deep inside him—an elemental emotion that he usually controlled easily. "You've been moving stiffly.... You're sore," she said gently as he placed the flat of his hand on the door and pushed slightly. "I'll get Leroy," she volunteered when he didn't move, blocking out the Montana night behind him.

"You just do that," he said softly, in a tone that raised the hair on the back of her neck. Then he stepped into her house.

She could have easily resisted his gentle push on the door. Instead she said, "Come in."

Wyatt looked around her living room, where Leroy had installed himself on the rug in front of the fireplace. The porker was fast asleep, snoring occasionally.

"He's exhausted," Tallulah whispered. "Maybe you'd better let him stay the night."

Wyatt's snort was short and disgruntled. He gazed down at her and said tightly, "*I* am the one with the aching muscles, Tallulah Jane, and I haven't been sleeping that well, either."

In her small living room, Wyatt's masculinity was framed and heightened by antiques, lace and doilies and braided rugs. He spread his legs like an Old West gunfighter ready for a showdown.

He looked at her trampoline and the aerobic mat in front of the television set. "You have excess energy," he stated darkly, as if she'd committed a crime.

Tallulah clasped her hands. Wyatt had sacrificed for the win of her team and had played very well after her yelling incident. He had played methodically, with a grim determination that almost frightened her, and now she realized how his efforts must have cost him. "I suppose I could give you a liniment rubdown. Would that help?"

Jack had never let her tend him and she waited for Wyatt to dismiss her offer.

"I'd really appreciate it," he murmured formally. "Where do you want me?" he asked, looking hopefully up the stairs to her bedroom.

"Do you want to talk about it?" Fallon whispered to Tallulah the next morning as she slid Mac Johnson's favorite breakfast platter of biscuits and gravy in front of him.

Tallulah shivered as she heard Wyatt rumble something to Norm in the kitchen, where the two were happily flipping pancakes and sharing recipes for fruit syrup and honey butter.

This morning he exuded a cheerful attitude, despite moving a little stiffly. He didn't seem like a man who had spent the night on her couch, but rather like a little boy who had gotten his toy train from Santa Claus and who was expecting a new gold-trimmed red caboose any minute.

Tallulah wiped the milk she'd spilled on the counter and shook her head as Fallon watched. The younger woman grinned.

"He's cute. You two are so suited for each other. He's the only man to tell you that you're a grump in the morning and to sit there and drink your herbal tea until you're in a sweeter mood. You absolutely glowered at him when he told you that you were frightening the customers. When he kissed you to stop you from arguing, you looked pole-axed."

Terror scurried through Tallulah.

Wyatt had seemed too relaxed in her house, looking with interest at her bedroom this morning. He had smiled slightly when she'd scooped the blankets high to her neck.

Being shy of Wyatt prowling around her bedroom at dawn and feeling slightly nauseated at the same time had been unnerving.

He had strolled around the ruffled, lacy interior of her home, touched the dried rosebud wreath with a fingertip, then studied the family pictures on her bureau. Scents of a freshly showered male body had swirled around the small room. She'd noted a bead of water clinging to the gray hair on his chest....

Wearing only his jeans and his morning beard, Wyatt was very dangerous and appealing.

"I fixed the leak under your sink," he said thoughtfully, peering out the curtains of her window to the dawn. Then he'd turned to her and his eyes had darkened, locking with hers until her throat dried.

"I love you," he had said. "A few years ago, I would have been dreaming about having children with you... adopting them, sharing our lives with them. About lying in that bed with kids coming in to sleep with us when it stormed. But now I'd settle for a second piece of pie," he added whimsically, as though to himself. "Or an invitation into that bed."

In another heartbeat, Wyatt was gone, taking Leroy with him back to his camper.

Tallulah shook her head— Jack had disdained household upkeep, staying in bed with her until late in the day or adopting children....

Wyatt fitted into her life very effectively. The thought frightened her; she was safe now, layered by the freedom she had worked so hard to achieve. Wyatt was slowly ripping away her safety....

Her fingers went cold and she realized she'd been gripping the countertop with all her might. She forced a bright smile for the Johnsons, who were settling into the corner booth.

"Blueberry," Norm was saying.

"Hot weather...temperature is rising today..." Fallon murmured, scooping her hair back from her face and lashing it on top of her head.

Without the mass of dark curls almost camouflaging her face, Fallon looked remarkably familiar. The angle of her forehead curved down to her eyebrows; her cheekbones slashing upward—

"Clover honey is better," Wyatt said as he left the kitchen and bumped into Tallulah, who was staring at Fallon.

Tallulah dragged her gaze to Wyatt's freshly shaven face. She studied the bone structure, and the lift of his black eyebrows over his eyes, which slanted slightly at the corners just as Fallon's did.

She studied Fallon's feminine mouth and compared the soft shape with Wyatt's grim one—

Wyatt's expression darkened as Tallulah slowly turned back to Fallon, studying her harder. "You...ah...you..."

"Let's get out of here," Wyatt said ominously, taking her hand and pulling her out of the café.

Tallulah locked her legs and grabbed a lamppost with her free hand. "Wyatt?"

He nodded to the sheriff, who was sitting in his patrol car and looking at them curiously. "Come along, Tallulah. I'll explain everything."

"You are Fallon's long-lost, worthless, shiftless father," she stammered as they passed the dry-goods store.

"Uh-huh. Not a very flattering description."

"You look exactly alike," she stated, staring at him as they passed her father's sporting-goods store.

"She's a lot prettier," he muttered, striding so fast that she almost had to lope to keep up with him.

Chelsea Jones yelled across the street and asked Wyatt if the browns, the rainbows or the brook trout were biting better.

"Try up at the north bend, where the ripples are on the west bank," he returned, pulling Tallulah along as she continued to study him.

"You are Fallon's father," she stated again as Wyatt's hand on the small of her back pushed her gently into her house.

"I am that," he said grimly, and sank into her large overstuffed chair with the air of a man who knew his world was crumbling under him.

He stared down at his hands and looked so lonely that Tallulah sank to her knees and touched his face. She ached for the pain he carried, whispering, "Wyatt, tell me...."

His pain became hers, the tears dripping slowly from her eyes. Inching closer, she sat on his lap and drew his head against her breast. She wrapped him in her arms, resting against him as he told of his searches, the lives wasted because of lies as he hunted for his daughter...of how he found her and began creating the safety that was Elegance.... He laid out his plan to introduce himself gently into Fallon's life, to get her to know him before explaining his identity—

Tallulah rocked him against her, wishing she could ease the pain. "You're not a rat...or a skunk," she whispered against his throat. "You were looking for her all the time. Oh, Wyatt.... That's the saddest, most beautiful story I've heard in my entire life."

Wyatt's arms tightened and his body shifted beneath hers. He tipped up her face to kiss the tears on her cheek. "I am truly glad you care, Tallulah Jane," he said in his soft Georgia drawl, and kissed her tenderly.

Then he watched her carefully from behind the shield of his lashes and said slowly, "I've been meaning to tell you— my family is arriving on Saturday. They're coming to see Fallon and Miracle...and to meet you. They think we're betrothed."

Six

"**Y**ou rat . . . you skunk. . . ." Tallulah muttered weakly as Wyatt sat beside her on her bed and patted the chilled, damp cloth across her forehead.

She sank against the pillow. Discovering Fallon's identity, Wyatt's approaching relatives, a nonexistent engagement and losing her breakfast within seconds was just too much.

She'd had a glimpse of Wyatt's expression before he had carried her upstairs. While he was bearing her five-foot-eleven body as though it were as fragile and tiny as Miracle's, Wyatt's face had been pale with stark fear.

She remembered Jack's contempt for sickly women and weakly batted Wyatt's hand away as he smoothed back the hair from her cold, damp cheek. She didn't want Wyatt to see her at her weakest, without her defenses. She'd learned a long time ago to shield herself— "Go away, Wyatt Remington. I am—"

"Angry? Sick?" he offered softly in a concerned tone.

"Mad." She shook aside the cold washcloth he'd flopped over her brow and glared up at him.

"You're upset," he murmured in a wise, perceptive tone.

"Mad," she repeated darkly, trying to escape the woozy feeling so she could have a really good go at him. "You should have told me."

Wyatt looked uneasy and she realized he'd been holding her limp hand. She jerked it away, placed it on her rolling stomach and continued glaring at him. "We made love three weeks ago," she stated. "Before we did, we determined we both are not usual reach-out-and-grab-it people. Lovemaking was an unusual occurrence for both of us. We must have trusted each other to a certain extent. Honesty is a big part of a relationship, don't you think?" she demanded.

Then she recalled what Wyatt had said moments ago and asked fiercely, "Betrothed? As in bespoken? Engaged?"

"It's an old-fashioned word for how I feel." Wyatt's broad shoulders looked as if he were carrying enough weights for ten men, but his eyes locked with hers.

Despite her mood, Tallulah felt the quick, deep jerk of her heart aching for him. "I'm not snuggling you or cuddling you," she said aloud. "Don't give me that orphan-pup look."

His eyebrows shot up. "Orphan pup?"

She wished the bed would stop rocking and said so. "Hold still, or I'll be sick again."

"I'm calling a doctor," Wyatt stated grimly, and began to rise.

Despite a fresh wave of nausea, Tallulah gripped Wyatt's hand. He wasn't leaving her. Not now, when he'd stepped into her safe life and ripped it to smithereens. She needed the safety of his fingers locked with hers; for now he was her anchor, the jerk. "No. You are sitting here and taking your medicine. Why didn't you tell me?"

"You hit me faster than a hungry trout takes a good lure," he said flatly. "The stream got too deep and ran too fast for a good cast— I wanted to work up to telling you about Fallon and Miracle. I was afraid you'd think I was all that Fallon thinks I am before I had a chance to prove myself."

"So all that business about her inheriting the house and a small income from some deceased, quirky relative—her benefactor—was just so much malarkey? You actually held me and whispered those things and *didn't tell me?*" she demanded, outraged.

Wyatt shifted restlessly, locked his jaw and looked at her as if expecting to be tossed out of her window. "Elegance is safe. My daughter and granddaughter needed to be safe. I checked out the town, had it investigated and visited here."

"Safe...." Tallulah pondered the word. Elegance was safe; Wyatt was not safe from her. "Don't you tell me you love me," she said warily as he looked down at her tenderly.

"Do," he returned firmly, and she groaned, closing her eyes.

"Lie down here and hold me," she ordered weakly, needing him near in her shifting, torn-apart world. "No rocking me...."

"What about snuggling?" he asked in that Southern drawl as he lay down carefully and drew her into his arms. Tallulah fitted her head to his chest and listened to the rapid *thump-thump* while Wyatt stroked her hair, his body tense. She sensed a deep fear running through him as he asked, "Just a little bit? A kiss on the forehead, like a little stamp to send away the woozies?"

"What do you want from me?" she asked carefully, fear surging through her. She turned her head to eye him. She suspected that Wyatt, when he set his mind to it, could charm old Mrs. Phinnis, who hated kittens and puppies.

"Commitment," he answered in that same heartbeat. "You don't have to love me. I'll take what I can get in that department. But you are not passing me off on another woman." He leveled a typical Gothic-guy glower at her.

He didn't frighten her. Anyone who would watch "Miss Swine the Divine" with Leroy couldn't be all bad. "Huh. That would be cruelty. Your skills aren't exactly up to par. If they were, you would have told me about Fallon and Miracle, poor things."

Then she frowned, remembering his haunted past. "Oh, Wyatt...all the time you've hunted for them.... Fallon thinks her father beat her mother and ran off with another woman." Tallulah reached slightly to hug Wyatt; he had endured so much. Then she fell back to the safety of her pillow.

"Thanks to her mother. And I don't want your sympathy," Wyatt said grimly.

"I don't think I was designed for the yin-and-yang bit," Tallulah whispered uneasily. "I failed that role before."

"You're perfect for me," Wyatt stated after kissing her forehead.

"A man doesn't keep secrets from his—"

"Sweetheart? Lover? Fiancée?"

"Making love once, three weeks ago, does not qualify you as my lover or my betrothed," Tallulah murmured as sleep weighted her. On the heels of a sleepless night, the morning had overpowered her. Then she yawned and said aloud, "I wonder now if there really is a big one with my name on it."

"Oh, there is. He's waiting for you. We'll talk about it when you're feeling better," Wyatt soothed.

He yawned slowly and turned her carefully on her side away from him, then drew her back tight against him. "Let's take a nap, Tallulah," he said in a deep, sleepy voice, as though he'd taken morning naps with her for years, and gathered her closer.

"I am going to the café," Tallulah stated unevenly the next morning as Wyatt pushed her back onto her bed.

"You stay put."

She eyed him, disliking his commanding tone and the way he tugged the daisy-spattered sheet up to her chin. He tucked her in, and unused to being fluttered over, Tallulah grumbled, "It's a passing flu."

"You're overworked and overtired. You turned white last night at the volleyball practice. That was after you went bicycling around the school track with Miracle on the back seat."

"Fern McKinsey was discussing how to sauté liver and bacon in wine. That would make anyone a little white— taking out veins and... You didn't have to carry me off the gym floor," she whispered, lifting her face to the cold washcloth he was patting over her forehead. "People will talk about you staying the night."

Wyatt slashed her a look that said the couch wasn't where he wanted to install himself and that they had passed certain landmarks in their relationship. Like making love for the first time. "I can handle the restaurant.... By the way, we're baby-sitting Miracle tonight. Fallon is taking your place at the starting softball league. The first practice is tonight and then the team is having an organizational meeting."

"I pitch," Tallulah said triumphantly. "The team needs my slow ball."

"You're not throwing anything until you feel better. You can coach her this afternoon after work. While you're sitting in the shade on the back-porch swing. Miracle can watch Leroy, and I'll catch. We're having barbecue—hamburgers. You've got a honey of a grill going to waste. Your dad is bringing over his ice-cream makings. I'll bring home ice for the bucket—"

"Humph. What do you know about catching?" Tallulah asked with disdain, and tried not to think about red meat on the grill, oozing greasy juices into the flames. Or the milk and eggs and sugar stirred by the paddles of the ice-cream freezer . . . waves of sweet, gooey stuff—

Wyatt leered at her, a shocking, eyebrow-lifting leer that could have charmed the coldest heart. "I know I'd like to catch a certain long-legged lady and make her mine until she asks for mercy."

Tallulah decided she should hold her own against his leer; she wasn't letting him get ahead of her. Wyatt would take that victory and run with it. There would be no stopping him.

"Do tell," she cooed, batting her lashes at him and wondering when the flirt in her had appeared.

That evening, Tallulah sat in her backyard swing and watched Fallon and Wyatt practice ball. Fallon glowed with excitement, studiously taking advice from Tallulah about a power-ball windup and a slow curve. Wyatt, in the catcher's crouch, encouraged Fallon with an easy deep voice that bore his pride.

Usually in the midst of activity, Tallulah wouldn't have interfered for the biggest trout in the stream.

Leroy oinked his comments and allowed Miracle to chase him merrily. Tallulah's father treated the evening as a landmark event, beaming widely as he indicated that he was glad another man had taken his daughter to hand. He and Wyatt grilled hamburgers and talked about burying stink bait, which caused Tallulah's stomach to roll.

She eyed the lure in her father's hat, the black-and-red colors catching the late-afternoon sun. The Tallulah lure had a distinct look to it, just a delicate, tantalizing mix of chenille and fur tied in a special way—tiny wings quivering and dancing almost erotically. . . .

Later, when Wyatt read to Miracle and rocked her to sleep, Tallulah fought the tears welling in her eyes.

Then Fallon stopped by the house, all glowing and excited about the team choosing her to play first base. Apparently Stan Redmond had an excellent slow pitch, which he'd been hiding, and the team was pleased to have him. Tallulah chewed on this news while Fallon reached up to hug Wyatt and kiss his cheek. He shattered quietly, standing very still long after Fallon had driven off with Miracle, who wouldn't go without Leroy.

Wyatt swallowed several times and blinked rapidly. His fists curled and uncurled at his sides as though he needed to wrap his arms around his family and keep them close.

"Everything is coming along according to your plan. She's getting to know you," Tallulah said gently, holding his hand as he continued to stare off into the night. A father without a family to hold was an aching sight, Tallulah decided. Tonight, with his plans taking shape, Wyatt needed to be comforted and to be kept active. She locked her arm around Wyatt's waist and snuggled closer. "Come along to bed now, Wyatt. You've had a hard day," she whispered, tugging him back into her house.

He wasn't escaping to his little camper trailer, there to watch "Miss Swine the Divine" for the night. That would be too lonely for words.

"What's this?" Wyatt asked huskily as Tallulah drew him up the stairway to her bedroom.

"I thought you might want to tell me about the big one...you know, how to lure him to my hook," she said softly against his throat before she pushed him into her bed. He sprawled gloriously, lying on his back and looking delicious in his jeans and T-shirt.

The summer breeze flirted through the lacy curtains at the window when he drawled sexily, "I've been meaning to talk to you about that."

The room stilled as he looked at her through the shadows. "Thank you for tonight," he said softly, the drawl wrapping around her heart. "For letting my family become a family here in your home," he said simply, lifting his hands to cradle his head.

"You're welcome," she said primly, suddenly nervous of him. "I think I'll just take a shower now."

"You do that and I'll take mine after you," he said unevenly. "I'll check to see that the lights are out and that the doors are locked."

"No one locks their doors in Elegance," she reminded him.

"Well. Let's just say that tonight—if you're feeling better—there's a reason why your doors should be locked tight," Wyatt murmured huskily. And a little trickle of heat started quivering low in Tallulah's stomach.

"I'm feeling better," she stated firmly. Tallulah shivered through her hot shower and while she applied powders and lotions that she'd never opened since last Christmas. She wanted everything to be new for Wyatt, and she fought the fear stabbing, fought the damage that Jack had done with his cutting words and disdainful looks. "Oh, Wyatt Remington, you have really stepped into a cow pile now. I fear I cannot show you mercy for raising what was dead . . . or for beginning what was never lit before you. . . ."

Tallulah slipped on her nightshirt and wished she had a lacy affair with which to vamp him so that he wouldn't think of any other woman before her.

"Betrothed . . ."

Oh, Lord. What if he looked at her and didn't want her?

Ugly memories went scurrying through her mind as she slid back to the bedroom, gripping her tattered rose chenille robe tight to her chest where the buttons were missing and her heart was pounding.

Wyatt was downstairs; she heard him moving through the house, the creak of the back door as he opened it to look out at the night— *Was he leaving her?*

Her throat dried, almost closing with fear as she thought about another man who had rejected her loving.

Wyatt's footsteps rose up the stairs and Tallulah dived into bed, gripping the covers to her throat. He walked to the bathroom and began showering. Tallulah arranged herself this way and that on the small old bed and finally decided that a woman waiting to entice a man might want to strip off the old robe. She ripped it away frantically and stuffed it under the bed.

He stood at the doorway. The moonlight crossing into the room outlined his tall body, and heat leaped within her. "Get into this bed, Wyatt Remington," she whispered firmly.

"Yes, ma'am," he murmured as he padded toward the bed and eased under the sheet beside her.

"You smell good," she ventured after a while when he did not move.

He looked at her in the dark, turning his head on the lacy pillowcase. "So do you. Tomorrow I'll fix the leak in the bathroom sink and get a bar of soap for your shower that doesn't smell like lilacs."

He was making plans, laying her choices before her to rummage through, to take or to leave. "You do that," Tallulah said slowly, and knew that she wanted him in her home. "Norm would be sure to notice. He says his nose has been sensitized lately and that he can pick out odors exceptionally well—"

She stopped breathing when Wyatt's big, rough hand skimmed her thigh lightly. He squeezed gently.

"What are you wearing under this sheet?" she asked desperately, shocked when she realized she had spoken her uppermost thoughts.

"I'm naked as a jaybird," he drawled in a tone laced with humor. "Lying here in my lilac-soap scents and waiting for you to attack me."

She breathed hard, aware that Wyatt was settling down for the night, yawning hugely and stretching until he caused her bed to shrink. "Just how do you feel about that—about a woman making the first move?" she asked cautiously, reined in by Jack's censure of wanton wives.

Wyatt laughed aloud. The deep rich sound started as a rolling chuckle, then erupted into full laughter. "I'd be mighty pleased," he said when he could. "And I would try to rise to the occasion."

She glanced quickly down the sheet covering his body and wondered where to begin....

"Kisses are always appropriate," Wyatt offered in a serious tone, turning his head to hers. "I shaved with your little bitty lady razor just so you could kiss away and not get scraped."

She eased her lips against his experimentally, then lay back to look at him and wonder how this night had all come about.

"Get this straight, Miss Tallulah Jane. I am not your exhusband," Wyatt said tightly. "I won't ever push you away or leave you when you need me. I'll tend your needs as carefully as I can."

The words rang out like a promise, striking so deep in her heart that it ached painfully.

She kissed him again just once, then before he changed his mind, she latched herself to him in a flurry of legs and arms and quick, hungry kisses. Wyatt stripped away the tangled sheet between them and drew her over him, his hands caressing up and down the length of her back and lower, cupping her intimately against him as he groaned raggedly. "Tallulah," he whispered harshly, answering her fevered kisses as the heat began to build between them.

His mouth was hot and wild, making her forget everything but her hunger for him. "You sure you won't melt, Wyatt?" she asked shakily against his throat, where she was nibbling on his slightly damp skin, then flicking it with her tongue.

"Lord Almighty," he gasped sharply. "I will strive to survive."

Tallulah smiled, then found herself giggling at his old-fashioned term. She wiggled against him, finding what she wanted, trapping and warming him between her thighs. The thin layer of silk separating them caused Wyatt to groan and he ran his fingertips along the elastic at her bottom, tantalizing her as they kissed.

"I'll just take this off," she whispered as she straddled him in the moonlight and tugged away her nightshirt. The wild, bold passion she had never allowed to escape surged from her in a heartbeat.

His gaze worshiped her, his dark hands slowly rising to cover the pale shape of her breasts, to mold and cherish them. He slowly lowered her to his mouth, gently kissing and suckling her.

"I hope you are a strong man, Wyatt Remington, and that you have lived right," she said quietly.

Wyatt eased the small package from where he had placed it by the bedside and she blushed as she realized he was preparing for her, for the passionate lovemaking she had shared with no one else. She watched, fascinated, as his hands trembled, failing to accomplish his intimate task the first time, the failure endearing him to her.

"I'm a bit nervous," he explained unevenly. "I want tonight to be perfect."

Wyatt lay there beneath her quivering thighs like a man who needed to be tasted, to be loved until all the aching shadows of his life slid away. His big, rough hands stroked her thighs gently, trembling and warm. She'd never been allowed to explore, to look at and to ponder over the reality of a man's body.

In fact, she'd been made to feel ashamed of her wildest desires—of positions and speaking her emotions and needs aloud . . . and now, Wyatt's hungry, smoldering look urged her on.

Tallulah smoothed the hair on his chest, rested her palm over his heavy heartbeat and allowed herself to explore him.

MORE GOOD NEWS FOR SUBSCRIBERS ONLY!

When you join the Reader Service, you'll also get our free monthly Newsletter; featuring author news, horoscopes, competitions, special subscriber offers and much more!

◄ TEAR OFF AND POST THIS CARD TODAY! ◄

Harlequin Mills & Boon
FREEPOST
P.O. Box 70
Croydon
Surrey
CR9 9EL

"We've got all the time in the world, sweetheart," he murmured as she moved experimentally above him, struggling frantically with her panties.

She wanted to be a part of him. To be locked with him, to step into that wonderful feeling of being richly loved—

Wyatt tore away her panties easily and helped her guide herself down onto him.

She hadn't meant to be swept away with the passion ripping through her.

But she did, moving frantically upon Wyatt and casting away the past with a fervor that heightened to the rhythm of the creaking bed—

The bed crashed to the floor while she thrashed upon Wyatt, unwilling to leave him just yet. He groaned and caressed and Tallulah heard a familiar sound outside their world of heat and glory—

"The doorbell is ringing..." she whispered against Wyatt's warm ear, closing her hands over his on her breasts. She stilled her quivering body, enclosing his arcing one.

"Doorbell? No, that's me, honey," he said tightly. "We're just about to the bell-ringing stage—"

She lifted her head, listening as the doorbell rang again and Wyatt groaned and shuddered and arched, his expression that of a man strained to his limits.

He lay there in the fallen bed, tangled in the sheets, as Tallulah scampered up and tugged her chenille robe from under the mattress. "Let it ring, Tallulah," Wyatt ordered darkly, and groaned again.

She flushed when she looked down at him in the moonlight.

She was guilty of desiring him right down to her bones, to the very depths of her heart. She'd been caught slaking herself upon him and— Tallulah gripped the robe tighter and scurried out of the room and down to the front door. She glanced at the clock over the mantel, and was surprised to discover that it was only ten p.m.

Tallulah began to tremble. She'd been frolicking with Wyatt for over an hour, testing and exploring and delighting. The thought knocked her sideways; Jack was very wrong. People did play and enjoy lovemaking and tasting and touching, and they enjoyed listening to their hearts flutter like one, reveled in the joining of their bodies and souls. She shuddered and gripped the doorknob as her legs weakened.

Cautiously she opened the door. "Yes?"

Four tall women stood on her doorstep, the fishing lures on their hats gleaming under the porch light. They were dressed in gaudy, tourist-looking shirts and jeans. Each battered hat had a Tallulah lure quivering in sexy black-and-red colors.

"You must be Tallulah," one of the women said firmly, and all of them smiled down at her. "You look absolutely like Wyatt's creation. All rosy and cute— Doesn't she look sweet, sisters?"

Tallulah cleared her throat. "Ah...do you know Wyatt?"

She'd been caught with him—the evidence sprawled upstairs in her fallen bed, looking as if he could strangle whoever had rung the bell.

"He's our sweet baby brother. We checked at his trailer after we went fishing in that gorgeous stream. Caught our limits, too, every one of us," the older woman with gray hair said in a soft Georgia drawl.

She peered hopefully over Tallulah's shoulder. "Ah, would baby brother happen to be here?" Then her eyes lit and she said, "Why, there he is, our little, sweet baby brother."

"'Evenin', Pearl," Wyatt said as he placed his hand on Tallulah's waist and his fingers caressed the faded chenille leisurely. His expression was very grim. "'Evenin', Ruby Mae...Jade...Dora Belle."

His sisters scanned his bare chest, his jeans unsnapped at the waist and his bare feet. Soulful eyes so like his own moved over him slowly; the cheekbones that Fallon shared with him were stamped on every sister.

"You're a night early and not welcome right now," he said tightly, and began to close the door.

Tallulah gripped it and tugged it away from him despite his resistance and deep scowl down at her. "I'm glad to meet you," she said, and invited them into her home.

"I don't suppose you'd have a back porch where we could clean our catch?" Ruby Mae asked politely in her softly accented voice.

"Hell, no," Wyatt returned flatly, glaring at their warm smiles. "Don't you each have a tribe of husbands, children and grandchildren to tend to? About thirty miles back the road you'll find a hotel. Use it. Then tote yourselves on home and bake a sweet-potato pie. You can mail it to me."

The sisters weren't at all intimidated, each hugging him and kissing and patting his cheek. Wyatt suffered, looking so much like a pampered and beloved Gothic guy that Tallulah grinned. "You're staying with me. I've got four bedrooms," she said as Pearl began to sniff at Wyatt's cheek and he moved warily away.

"Wyatt Sebastian-honey, since when have you started using lilac toilet water?" Pearl asked gently. "Is that a new man in-thing to do? Some new male fashion?"

Tallulah gazed at him and pressed her lips together, fighting a smile. "'Wyatt Sebastian-honey'?"

"Tallulah..." Wyatt began in his best threatening tone.

"Go along now, Wyatt. Take them to the back porch, where they can clean their catch," she said, trying not to giggle at his outraged expression.

"The fish are in the back of the van, honey," Dora Belle said. "Would you mind getting them?"

"He's such a darling boy. Always was," Ruby Mae murmured as they all watched Wyatt stalk down the steps toward the van.

"Until that she-polecat got him and twisted his guts inside out by taking away his baby and dragging her all over the world," Dora Belle added.

Ruby Mae looked at Tallulah worriedly. "Do you know about Wyatt's search for his baby? Oh, dear, sisters, maybe we've stepped in a cow pile, bursting in upon baby brother and letting out his secrets—"

"I know about Fallon," Tallulah murmured. "But no one else does. The time hasn't been right."

"That she-wolf who took her away—" Dora Belle began darkly, and Tallulah saw the angry, raw power that this family could raise from the depths of their loving hearts. Especially when a member of their clan was hurt.

"That's all over now, Dora Belle," Pearl soothed. "His wandering days are over. He's found his baby girl, and something else, I'd wager," she added, as all the tall women looked down at Tallulah.

"She's sweet," Pearl said, wiping her tears away from her eyes.

"You're just perfect," Ruby Mae said, kissing Tallulah's flushed cheek. "Now I can see why Wyatt has created his best lure. The Tallulah is just a perfect image of you. Sweet, feminine… My, and she smells like the lilacs blooming back home in Georgia."

"Your offer of spending the night is just ever-so welcome," Pearl murmured. "Ah, would you mind showing us where the ladies' room is?"

Tallulah led them upstairs to the larger bathroom. The sisters exclaimed over her lovely, snug home as they went, and suddenly Tallulah realized they were silent. She paused, holding the stack of towels she had just taken from her linen closet, and turned to see all four women standing in front of her bedroom door.

The evidence was sprawled all over the room. The scene of her loving-Wyatt event ran from her nightshirt tossed on top of the bureau to the sheets and blankets tangled everywhere. The fallen bed was exhibit number one. Exhibit number two, the silver foil packet, caught the moonlight from the window and shot a myriad of colors through the dark room.

"My," Pearl breathed.

"Lordy," Dora Belle said unevenly, her hand to her heart.

"'Good golly, Miss Molly,'" Ruby Mae whispered, quoting Little Richard's rock-and-roll song title.

Then they all turned to beam at her. "Wyatt has given his heart," Jade said softly.

Tallulah realized suddenly that this sister had not spoken until now.

"Jade never says anything until it needs saying. She's been that way since she was a widow at an early age. Her dear departed Henry had complained of her chattering," Pearl explained gently. She hustled the sisters along to the bathroom. "We'll just be a minute...."

Tallulah dressed in two seconds, closed the bedroom door after her and found Wyatt grumbling near the back porch. "You're gutting those fish with a vengeance," she began gently.

He paused to glare at her, then began his sword-swishing, expert fish-cleaning technique again.

Then Tallulah started to laugh—the happiness stirring right out of her into the starlit night....

Because Wyatt looked so disgusted, she went to stand behind him. She wrapped her arms around him, stood on tiptoe to brace her chin on his shoulder and kissed him with the tenderness she felt in her heart. Wyatt's lips were gentle when he said, "You know I've got fish guts on my hands. Otherwise I'd carry you off from that herd of invading magnolias. I'd hitch my pickup to the camper and pull you off into some secluded pine grove, there to make love until the steam melted the trailer seams. I am not a happy man, Tallulah. I've been foiled. I hadn't gotten to the part where I tell you I love you yet. You rushed me, and now *they're* here. You'll pay for answering the doorbell when I told you not to.''

She thought about Wyatt's steaming camper and grinned up at him. Because he looked so nettled, she hugged him tighter. Wyatt groaned, moving his back against her breasts as she asked, "If you pirated me away in your steaming camper, what would we do with Leroy?''

Wyatt answered with a short, flat snort that said he wasn't thinking of Leroy's comfort at the moment.

Seven

"You know, Wyatt Sebastian-honey," Pearl murmured three days later as she cast upstream and watched the Tallulah float down the ripples. The second week of July was cool, the fishing good, and the sisters were thrilled with their catches. Wyatt wished the fish weren't biting and that he could return to Tallulah's bed, as Pearl continued, "You're not too old to consider having another sweet little baby. You missed so much as a daddy."

Wyatt's arm stopped in the middle of his cast; a trickle of uneasiness went up the back of his neck. He'd been locked in his thoughts concerning Tallulah's mysterious nausea when she sniffed certain odors. He'd thought for hours about one thing—the possibility of a baby.

Fear and joy tormented him in equal doses.

They'd made love too fast that one time; Tallulah had taken him quickly, too quickly. She couldn't have conceived in that one flurry of lovemaking—

A baby. Wyatt squinted against the morning sunlight and cherished the thought, turning it and finding himself smiling with quiet golden delight.

He hadn't been allowed to share his first baby, to experience the miracle that would become his child— He swallowed and remembered the times he'd wanted to place his hand on his ex-wife's expanding stomach and had been denied.

The next instant he was terrified, fearing Tallulah's reaction if the baby was a reality.

Leroy grunted and rooted, performing his cheerleader imitation in his special woodland flower patch. His beady eyes gleamed with pleasure; he had been cuddled and pampered by the four sisters, Tallulah, Fallon and Miracle. Like a pasha with a harem, Leroy ruled Tallulah's house and remained entrenched there, while Wyatt tried to sleep in his camper trailer parked in her backyard.

"I heard you tossing pebbles at the poor girl's window at three o'clock this morning, honey," Dora Belle said, reeling in her line for another cast. "She needs her sleep. Goodness, she's involved in everything in the community."

"Poor little thing. She hasn't ever been a mama. Not too late for her, either, Wyatt. You might consider how pleased she'd be if you'd mention that you'd like a family to raise. That you'd like to settle here, where her people are, and begin your life anew. You're making such strides with Fallon. She really likes you. I'll bet she's considering you to be her daddy already," Ruby Mae added, sliding Wyatt a cautious glance.

"If he's going to stay in town, he shouldn't embarrass either one of his ladies, and he should acquire some decent clothes and get a haircut," Jade said. "The way I see it, Wyatt's gypsy days are over."

He grimly continued fishing, giving casting advice when needed and trying to keep to himself when possible. The four sisters would not allow it. They had him and he knew it.

"We could tell your Tallulah was something special the moment you air-mailed us these prize lures," Pearl was saying. "The Tallulah is a statement of love if I ever saw one."

"Poor little sweet thing. When that fine daddy of hers was here and we fried our catch of the day, she got a bit weak. You were right to hold her on your lap and cuddle her, Wyatt. Poor thing just wilted all of a sudden...just stared at our sizzling skillet of fish and at the fried potatoes and wilted lettuce and black-eyed peas and drooped on the spot."

"Hasn't a clue what's in store for her," Jade murmured.

"My, she's a healthy girl. If she decided to be a mama at this point in her life, with all the modern miracles, there wouldn't be a thing to worry about."

"She's got a certain round look to her face—"

Wyatt glared at them and they blithely smiled back.

All except Jade, who continued casting leisurely. "Tallulah Jane is with child," she said in her soft firm voice. "She's got our Wyatt's child growing in her and she doesn't know it. I'd be working on that, Wyatt Sebastian-honey. Getting her used to the idea and marrying her. Try romancing her. Take lessons or something."

Pearl grinned widely. "He can't catch her. He's slow as molasses. Tallulah is a runner, quick on her feet and lively. She's a trophy catch if I ever saw one."

"Well, he caught her once, well and good, I'd say," Ruby Mae added with delight. "Our baby brother knows what he's about when he wants a keeper."

"When are you leaving?" Wyatt demanded darkly.

"Why, baby brother. Are we cramping your style?" Dora Belle asked, batting her lashes innocently.

Leroy continued grunting and rooting from the sidelines.

Wyatt tried not to run up the bank and straight to the Tall Order Café; he feared he'd lose Tallulah at any minute—especially when she discovered that she might be carrying his baby. If his sisters had noticed, other people would soon realize something had changed in her.

He gripped his rod too tightly, holding it and not working the Tallulah as she zigzagged merrily down the stream, untended by his hand. Just as Tallulah could do very easily. She'd shuffled off the exes without much strain.... He'd dealt with the fear of losing Fallon's trail for years, a gut-wrenching fear that had never left him for almost nineteen years— Now he was sweating every minute, dying with fear when Tallulah's hand rubbed her stomach and she looked woozy.

He loved her deeply.

There would never be another love in his heart.

What if Tallulah hated him? What if he lost her, the other half of his soul, his heart?

Fear tightened his chest and took his stomach to his throat.

"Don't you look so scared, baby brother," Pearl was saying gently. "Love will overcome."

"I'd like a baby," he said slowly, trying out the words for the first time with his sisters, who had changed his diapers and had known his secrets.

"'Course you would. You're a loving man, and don't sell Miss Tallulah Jane short, either. She knows a good catch when she sees one, mark my words," Jade remarked. "You'd better hurry up, Wyatt-honey. The next stage is when she sleeps at the drop of a hat. That's probably why she isn't answering your pebble tossing now. She's probably dead to the world... saving up her energy for carrying that sweet little baby nestling inside her."

Wyatt grinned widely, his heart tingling inside him.

"Look at him," Dora Belle was saying. "Six-foot-four of goofiness, loaded with rainbows and grins and love."

"Sweet little baby brother," Pearl was saying fondly.

"He'd better step on it and set the hook," Jade said flatly, using a fishing term that expressed keeping a fish once it was enticed. "Tallulah is a keeper for certain."

In the evening, Fallon cast into the plastic swimming pool that Tallulah had installed in her backyard for Miracle. Wyatt eased his arms around his daughter to show her how to work the fishing line in her left hand and the rod in her right one.

He closed his eyes, thinking of the last time he'd held Fallon and had clamped his lips closed to keep from telling her how pretty she was.... "Perfect...beautiful..." he said now, then added, "Good cast."

She beamed up at him. "You think so, Wyatt?"

He was nodding, locked in his thoughts. Fallon was as tall as the Remington stock, as fragile as the Southern women who had backbones of steel when needed. She'd shown her Remington blood and had survived hard times, protecting her young, his beautiful grandchild named Miracle.

Miracle came running in her blue polka-dot sunsuit and locked her arms around Wyatt's leg. "Up."

He swallowed heavily, then bent to lift the miniature copy of his daughter to his hip. He met her juicy kiss and melted; Miracle was what Fallon must have looked like, a mop of curls and eyes that said what she was thinking.

Was this what his child with Tallulah would look like? Wyatt studied the little wonder cuddling against him, her ruffled bottom perched on his forearm. He loved Miracle deeply, this tiny image of Fallon, whose life he'd never been allowed to share—

Fallon studied him in the evening light and Tallulah placed her arm around the younger woman's waist. "He's a very nice man," she said gently, and Wyatt kissed Miracle's exploring fingertips as he listened closely.

"I know. I've never known anyone like him," Fallon answered, her gaze locking with Wyatt's as she frowned slightly. Then her eyes skipped away shyly to the sisters who had come to fold Wyatt and Miracle within their soft midsts. "A family," Fallon whispered longingly. "My daughter needs a family like this one."

"We'll be your family," Pearl answered. "Miracle and you can have us if you want us."

Fallon swallowed and leaned slightly against Tallulah. Her eyes shimmered with tears and her lips quivered. "I've been through hard times. You might not want me."

He should have been there for her, and he wasn't—

Miracle unlatched one chubby arm from Wyatt's neck and held out her hand to her mother. "Mama."

The sisters looked at Wyatt; Jade touched his arm. "Fallon, there are secrets in everyone's life," Wyatt said gently. "You have to pick up the pieces and begin again sometimes. It looks to me you've made a good home for your daughter.... And you've found people who love you for what you are."

Fallon's slight body shook in Tallulah's arm and she turned to sob on Tallulah's shoulder. "We should go home," she murmured. "You'll be wanting to spend time alone as a family."

"You're not going anywhere," Tallulah said gently, rocking the girl against her and locking her eyes with Wyatt's. "We love you and Miracle and you're a part of our lives...."

Wyatt held Miracle closer and felt as if he were bleeding onto the lawn, aching with the need to hold Fallon and comfort her and tell her she was his own...how he had loved her and searched for her because love doesn't stop. "Love doesn't stop," he found himself whispering through a throat tightened by emotion. "It just goes on, Fallon, and gets stronger."

Dora Belle sobbed and ran to Fallon, followed by the other three sisters, who enfolded her in their arms and sweetness and tears. "You belong to us, Fallon Louise," Jade stated firmly, kissing Fallon's damp cheek. "So you have a family from this day forward, for ever and ever."

Fallon blinked away a tear. "How did you know my middle name was Louise?"

Jade glanced at the other sisters. Pearl stroked Fallon's curls and said firmly, "Our mother's name was Louise and you look a bit like her."

"I do?" Fallon's voice rang with happiness.

"Sure do. And you look like my children and all their cousins. So you see, when the Remington clan claims you, you're claimed well and good. You're a member of the family for your whole lifetime."

Miracle was practicing her hugging and Wyatt realized that a tear had slid from his lashes to his lips. He licked the salty taste and nuzzled Miracle's curly hair. "You'll be all right, Fallon," he said with his heart. "Just fine."

Later, the sisters and Tallulah took Miracle into the house to sing old hymns to her and rock her asleep. Fallon sat on the back-porch swing with Wyatt. His daughter was wrapped in loneliness and regrets and he ached for her.

"I want Miracle to have what I never did...a family around her. Mother had one goal in life and that was never to let my father see me. She's happy now, traveling the world with her new husband. But I wanted Miracle to have a home to grow up in. Whoever left me the house and has the lawyer deposit money in my bank account every month is a godsend," Fallon whispered above the call of the night birds. "Elegance is my very first home."

Wyatt inhaled, stemming the fear racing through him. "Have you ever thought that maybe your father might have searched for you? That he might have loved you?"

"Mother said he mistreated her. She didn't give me a home, packed me up at the drop of a hat and off we'd go across Europe with one of her boyfriends, then back to the States and off again.... But she loved me and I loved her, and my father hurt her."

Fallon dashed away a new round of tears and Wyatt swallowed tightly as he drew her slowly against his chest. "Things get twisted through the years. Whatever happened before, Fallon, you have a family now."

"You feel safe...."

She snuggled to his chest, and Wyatt tightened his arms around her, looking off into the bleak night. Telling her that he was her father now wouldn't do. He rocked her slender body and mourned for her loss.

And his own.

The minutes crept by and Fallon straightened slowly. "I am so embarrassed."

Wyatt wanted to tell her that she was his own, that he'd loved her from the first moment the nurses had shown her to him. That her mother had lied so that she wouldn't have to share Fallon— Pain sliced through him and his throat tightened....

Tallulah's familiar scent enfolded Wyatt and she slid down into the seat next to him. She smoothed the taut muscles in his neck, and when he looked at her, Wyatt did not attempt to shield his pain and helplessness. "Everything is going to be just fine," Tallulah said firmly before she lifted her lips to his.

Fallon shifted restlessly and Wyatt wrapped an arm around her and the other around Tallulah. "Let's just sit here awhile and swing and let my sisters fuss over Miracle and Leroy," he said. "You two can protect me from their plotting ways."

Fallon laughed merrily before each woman placed her head on Wyatt's shoulder and they listened to the night and the squeaking porch swing. "I'll have to oil that squeak," he said, kissing the top of each head.

"Shh, Wyatt. Tallulah is sleeping," Fallon whispered.

"I'm slowing up," Tallulah muttered darkly. "My meringue won't stand and my exes won't jitterbug with me anymore. I couldn't keep up if they did ask me. Maybe middle age has caught me."

Her breasts ached miserably and she attributed it to dreaming about Wyatt's fingers manipulating the tiny wings of his lures. Just one month ago, they'd made perfect love that would haunt her forever. She yawned and hungered for Norm's cherry cheesecake with a wedge of dill pickle. Wyatt tensed suddenly and she lifted her head to look at him.

When Wyatt's concerned expression turned to horror, she realized she had spoken her thoughts aloud. She glared at him. "I like cherries and I like pickles," she stated. "So what of it?"

He was watching her more closely than Fallon, and his sisters were sharing some sort of marvelous joke on him. Tallulah yawned again and pushed away the impulse to curl against Wyatt's hard, comfortable frame.

He'd been acting ornery. His sisters had tormented him unmercifully over a secret family joke and he bore a dogged look while they clustered gaily around him. Once Fallon had rescued him by asking him to help start her aged car and giving his diagnosis of its problem.

Two hours later at the evening volleyball gym practice, Tallulah watched Joanie Bell serve a fast one, low over the net with enough spin on it to bore through a wall.

That should be her out there, leading the town team on to glory, beating the neighboring town's team into the gymnasium's varnished floorboards. A captain of a volleyball team couldn't get a real grip on the game while sitting on the sidelines.

"Maybe I'm low on iron," she muttered after a yawn.

"Uh-huh," Wyatt said slowly. "Have you thought about taking up easier sports?"

"Nah. I've always been athletic." Then she yawned again.

"Right," Wyatt mumbled. Then he gave her a hot, dark look that reminded her of their passion that had been interrupted by his sisters.

Randy Newcomer trotted off the floor between sets to crouch in front of her. "Hey, Stretch, what's the scoop? Not feeling so good?" he asked, placing his hand on her forehead and searching her face.

She glared at him. "Get back in there and leave me alone."

Randy glanced over her head to Wyatt. "She never talked like that when *we* were dating," he said accusingly. "Haven't you been treating her right?"

Tallulah didn't have to look at Wyatt to see his scowl; she heard it in his low, ominous tone. "She gave you away, didn't she? Maybe I'm a keeper."

Tex Wilson trotted off the floor, dried himself with the team's battered towel and stood studying Tallulah intently. She'd matched him with Maizie Walters and now they were engaged, but Tex—a paramedic—kneeled to take her wrist and test her pulse. "Feeling a little down, Tallulah?"

"She's just fine," Wyatt muttered, taking Tallulah's hand in his own.

Tex, an ex-heavyweight boxer who lifted weights daily, measured Wyatt's frame, sheathed in a T-shirt and battered jeans. "She's special," Tex stated, meeting Wyatt's eyes.

"I'll come to softball practice next week," Tallulah said as Wyatt gritted his teeth and tightened his fingers on her wrist.

Tex shook his head and Randy grabbed the sweaty towel, wiping it over his chest. "You better take care of yourself," they said in unison.

"You're pretty pale and droopy. No volleyball or softball until you're looking better," Tex said firmly. "You look like you'd rather throw up on home plate than slide into it."

Wyatt placed his arm around her shoulders in a protective gesture, as if he was shielding her from harm. He appeared alarmed. "Slide? As in into home plate or first base?"

"She's the best slider we have. Can slide right under a catcher before he knows where she's at," Randy stated before they returned to the game.

Wyatt's breath whizzed by Tallulah's face as he inhaled sharply. His fierce expression took in the exes and then Tallulah. "She's taking up fishing," he said very slowly. "It's gentler."

Later, at her house, he pulled her into the coat closet. Wyatt ignored ribbons and scarves that spilled from a box he'd dislodged from the top shelf. He started kissing her in those delicate little come-play-with-me-honey kisses that melted her all the way to her toes. She ached for him in every fiber of her body and her soul. Shoving aside the hangers, Tallulah stood on tiptoe and wrapped her arms around him. "I missed you," he murmured against her hot cheek as his hand slid under her blouse to find her breast.

Her flesh lurched into his palm, aching for his caress.

Her legs quivered, her body dampening as she remembered the moment just before Wyatt's sisters had rung her doorbell.

Tallulah felt as juicy and succulent as an Idaho Sweet— Her response startled her, frightened her, and she gripped his shoulders tightly.

"Don't you pluck me like one of your lures, Wyatt Remington, or I just might—" She let out a high, keening sound that Wyatt smothered with another meltdown kiss. "We're not kids anymore, Wyatt," she muttered when she could speak and Wyatt was trembling and hot against her.

She noted distantly that she wasn't tired anymore, but that the heated excitement ripping through her was for Wyatt.

"Come out to the trailer," he whispered between nibbling her earlobes. "We'll watch 'Miss Swine the Divine.'"

She laughed against his throat, then bit him lightly. "My, how you do talk."

Wyatt held her close and slid his hand inside her jeans, spanning her stomach. "I'd like a baby with you," he said quietly above the sound of her rapidly beating heart. "What do you think about that?"

Tallulah went very still. "You mean adopt children? At our age?"

Wyatt placed his chin over her head and snuggled her close. She blew away a ribbon that had drifted from his shoulder to her nose. "Yes," he said firmly. "Let's get married right away and try for a while first. My little swimmers haven't been put to the test since Fallon was conceived years ago. Well, other than that time by the stream when you took me before I was ready for you."

Tallulah swallowed and blinked. "Swimmers?"

"You know...biology...male swimmers and female eggs—"

"Wyatt Remington!" she stammered, flushing wildly.

"It's a part of love," he said defensively. "And we haven't given me a real chance, now have we? I love you, Tallulah, and—"

"Swimmers," she repeated blankly, her hand pressing against her stomach. She closed her eyes and saw a school of tiny fish heading for a warm, dark nest—

He grabbed the doorknob that had been rattling and held it firmly as Pearl's soft voice called, "Is that you, Wyatt Sebastian?"

"Go away, Pearl-girl," he snapped. "I am romancing my sweetheart in the only little bit of the house you have left me. If you'd leave the countryside, I'd make better time."

A chorus of soft Southern feminine laughter rippled outside the door and Tallulah hid her hot face against his throat. "This is ridiculous," she muttered as he stroked her back with his free hand and kissed her forehead.

"What will you give me to run down to the restaurant for an order of Norm's cherry cheesecake with a pickle?" he asked with a sexy leer, and nudged away a coat sleeve from his shoulder. "If you lock your bedroom door tonight, I could climb that old trellis outside your window and deliver your desserts," he offered hopefully as Tallulah straightened her clothing and her hair.

She stood apart from him and reached to turn on the bald overhead light bulb. Above her, Wyatt looked rumpled and very hot. She lifted away a pink silk scarf from his shoulder, wrapped it around his neck and stroked the silky lengths over his hard chest. "I can't believe we are standing here in a closet and acting like this. Actually talking about swim— about the biology of making a baby."

"Get used to it," Wyatt said tenderly, then escorted her out of the mussed closet with the air of a country squire promenading his betrothed. He tossed a length of pink scarf over his shoulder with a flourish.

The sisters were waiting, hands clasped to their breasts, their eyes rich with tears. Pearl took away a scarf that clung to Tallulah's shoulder and plucked away a T-shirt that was draped down Wyatt's side.

"Baby brother is glowing," Jade stated as she studied Wyatt's pink scarf. "Glowing from ear to ear. Looks like an unholy toothy hyena. Or maybe he looks like a gator, ready to gobble this poor little girl."

"He's cute. Don't you pick on him, Jade," Dora Belle ordered gently.

"We're leaving in the morning, baby brother. But we'll be back before the snow flies to see what's new," Ruby Mae said cheerily before they enfolded Tallulah and began pampering her.

"Thank you, Lord," Wyatt muttered, and excused himself. A few minutes later he asked Tallulah if he might have a private word with her on the back porch. There he presented her with a cherry cheesecake topped by a pickle slice and received a sweet, loving, hungry kiss as a thank-you.

If she was carrying his child, she would nourish the baby from her body— A poignant ache, so sweet it bordered heaven, shot through him as he thought about Tallulah nursing their child. "I'll want something a bit more substantial the minute my clan leaves. I fear I have a dreadful hunger for you, my love," he whispered, folding her against him. He rocked her until they stopped trembling.

"My meringue is flat," Tallulah stated ominously the next morning. She slid a second slice of blackberry pie in front of Wyatt. Then she started sobbing quietly, ignoring the curious looks from the Tall Order's customers. "Onions," she explained as she wiped her eyes.

Wyatt stopped thinking about how sweet it would be to hold their baby and cuddle him and wake up for three a.m. feedings. He glanced at Tallulah's enlarged, pert bustline thrusting at her T-shirt and decided that maybe she would have to wake up, too.

She frightened him. His fear started the moment his sisters' van pulled out of her driveway this morning. Tallulah had yawned sleepily, blinked back tears and begun to cry quietly. Since then, Tallulah had been on the verge of tears.

Wyatt didn't know whether to hold her or not. He had cautiously drawn her into his arms, and she had sobbed for five minutes. Then she'd pushed back from him and sniffed. "Don't you say anything, Wyatt. I liked your family, even if you are a rotten lowdown skunk. It's a wonder to me why your sisters love you so much. You know very well that I'm emotional right now—some sort of midlife crisis— My house was so full of life and now they're gone— It's only seven o'clock in the morning and you ran them off."

She had leveled a glare at him through her tear-spattered glasses. She'd straightened them with a thrust of her finger and her frown had darkened. "Well, you did. And you're making me nervous with this strange look you keep giving me—like 'you *are* to take it easy.' Then there's you taking over at the Tall Order and the customers demanding your double-decker cheeseburgers. You're fixing things everywhere, and I can't tell what is working now and what's not…because some of what shouldn't be working is. I can't trust anything to work or not work, and I can't sleep sometimes and sometimes I can. It's all your fault," she had finished darkly, then marched off to the house and locked the door against him.

In the time that it took Wyatt to run his fingers through his hair and shake his head to clear it, she had unlocked the door and hurled herself into his arms. The instant after that, she was yawning and going limp in his arms. "I am tired," she had whispered against his throat, and snuggled closer to him.

Wyatt carried her into the house and up the stairs, all the time waiting for her snit to rush back. When it didn't, and Tallulah went right to sleep, he lay tensely beside her and held her. Gradually he drifted off to sleep.

An hour later Tallulah had awakened in a flurry and had rushed off to work, quite flustered with sleeping until eight a.m.

Uncertain how to approach this new side of the woman he loved, Wyatt had taken his time in coming to the Tall Order. He had carefully ordered coffee and pie. Now he sat very still and hoped he didn't say or do anything to upset Tallulah. The much-desired second piece of pie now sat in front of him.

He pondered the juicy blackberries and wondered if he should act happy and cheerful when Tallulah was near…or perhaps just wait and see which Tallulah mood the weather blew in—

Beside him now, Norm growled, "Do something, Wyatt. Tallulah's upset. Can't you smell the onions?"

By then Tallulah was steaming out of the café, carrying her tackle box and her fishing pole. "Be back this afternoon," she said airily as she passed Norm and Wyatt on her way to her pickup. "Fish are biting. My big one is waiting."

Wyatt studied the second piece of blackberry pie and decided that Tallulah was more important.

He found her casting wildly down at the stream. He settled onto a log and chewed a stalk of grass and ducked when her lure whizzed by his ear.

To have another baby, to hold his child in his arms, to burp it and to change diapers would be the sweetest thing in the world. Wyatt watched Tallulah drag her lures through the cattails and tug pine cones from trees as he thought about how much he had missed in Fallon's life. She hadn't started teething when Michelle had dragged her away. He'd missed Fallon's first step, her first word.

Wyatt swallowed, his chest tight with the heartbreak of the past and joyous with the new life that Tallulah might be nourishing in her long, lean body.

With two females—and Miracle as a third—wrapped so tightly in his life, each in a separate way, Wyatt knew he had to step carefully. The loss of any would be like a part of his heart torn away—

He closed his eyes, drifting with the dream of Tallulah having his child—

Just then she looked over her shoulder to him in a way that started his senses pumping. His muscles tensed and he swallowed. He'd had the same sensation just days before Fallon's mother had run away—

"You know, Wyatt . . . I've been thinking about your 'little swimmers' remark. I think they should be put to the test. If I'm suffering from some dreaded, mysterious disease, I may as well go all out."

Wyatt tried to breathe, forcing air into his lungs as she turned back to snaring pine cones and cattails. The world of dappled sunlight, skimming through the pine trees and catching the summer green of the thick brushes, hovered and stopped, like a raindrop poised to fall on the tip of a sword. He gripped the log with his fingertips as though he were clinging from the edge of a dangerous cliff... with hungry lions waiting below to have him for dinner. Wyatt struggled for balance. After a morning of tiptoeing around every word, he sensed his next words were critical. If he said the wrong thing... He cleared his throat and asked very carefully, "Ah... what do you mean?"

Then Tallulah began to cry while she cast rapidly and never came close to the stream. Her line flashed like a whip and Tallulah tugged free a stand of flowers from the bank. Bright yellow petals flew into the stream and swirled away.

Wyatt was on his feet, moving toward her, his fear for her lurching wildly. She pointed the rod at him and stopped him with a dark, fierce glare. "You look shocked... poleaxed. And afraid. You don't want me. I knew it."

Eight

Tallulah squashed the list of female candidates who might suit Wyatt. She tossed the crushed paper ball onto a heap of others and drew the blanket up to her eyes to wipe away her tears.

The thought of Wyatt naming a lure after another woman was just too much.

Tallulah crossed her arms over her aching breasts.

She couldn't concentrate on who would be a perfect match for Tracy Simmons, a widow for seven years. Elegance was Tallulah's town, the people counting on her matchmaking skills—and all she could think about was Wyatt.

"Well, he has certainly passed his matchmaking tests. I'll say that for Mr. W. R. Lures. Here I am ... thirty-eight and just possibly carrying his baby. I'd say he's passed his lessons, all right, and that his little swimmers know their business," she muttered, scratching off the name of Donna

Wheeler after she had jotted it down on a fresh piece of paper. "She's too sweet for him."

Tallulah closed her eyes and saw Wyatt sitting on the log, looking all broody and secretive as she fished. The wind caught his shaggy hair, tossing it seductively, and she ached to grip it in her fingers and draw his lips to her aching breasts.

She ached to have him tell her he loved her in that soft Southern drawl.

"You've picked a fine time to get heated up, Tallulah Jane," she chastised herself. "You'd better stop thinking about Wyatt's state just before his sisters came and interrupted him. You'll never get that close to him again. You've frightened him down to his boots."

Deep inside her a tiny round of quivers reacted instantly and she groaned long and slow. "I will not have him obligated to stay in one place or think he has to marry me," she muttered after a sniff. "He's been hiding out for the past three days, except for coming to the restaurant to eat. I will not run after him when he's holed up in the trailer or fishing by himself."

Tallulah eased away the blanket and studied the shape of her body. She looked at the drugstore pregnancy test lurking on her dresser and felt a wobbly smile grow on her lips. "Swimmers," she repeated slowly, thinking about how Wyatt had given himself to her that first time. At his sexual height, he was beautiful, primitive, strong and everything a man should be when he was making a baby—

He'd chased one daughter across the world. A man like Wyatt, set in his ways, would claim his babies and honor his obligations.

Tallulah wiped away her tears.

She placed her hands on her stomach, testing the soft shape and wondering about the baby. "You've picked a fine time, Tallulah," she said again. "Imagine sneaking out of town to race a hundred miles away to get a drugstore pregnancy test. Mr. Wilkins at the drugstore would have told the whole town one minute after you'd bought it here in Elegance."

Why couldn't she feel about Wyatt as she felt about the other men who had passed through her life?

Why couldn't she just pat him on that tight rear during a volleyball game the way she did the other guys?

Why couldn't she just match him with another woman, then slowly slide away from him as his new love entered his life?

Why couldn't she think of Wyatt as her buddy, her friend, who needed keeping for a time?

"I want you.... I love you...."

Her exes hadn't ever given her a red rose bouquet.

Not one of them had a porker for a best friend.

Her buddies hadn't mentioned swimmers or whispered of sensual delights as Wyatt had done.

Not one of her buddies, her exes, had attempted to claim her for himself, squiring her around with that possessive hand on the small of her back. She'd moved through life caring for others and no one had asked to take care of her....

Her exes danced fast, jitterbugging to the jukebox, but Wyatt moved slowly and surely—

Tallulah yawned and cursed Wyatt for complicating her life from the first moment she saw him.

She flopped over onto her stomach and instantly tensed when her tender breasts pressed against the mattress. She slipped a pillow beneath her and closed her eyes, allowing the late-afternoon breeze to calm her, swishing the curtains from her open window.

She eased her thigh over another pillow and studied the curtains. She moved her leg slowly upon the pillow and longed for Wyatt's hard, hair-roughened thigh.

She felt very sexual now, as if she could fly out of her window, find Wyatt and swoop down on him, taking him where she found him. She contemplated her late-developing sexuality and how Wyatt had started her motors humming, at an age when some women were becoming grandmothers.

Of course, Wyatt was already a grandfather, and he didn't seem slowed, even a little.

Until she'd broached the fear within her—that she might be pregnant—to him.

A big, worldly, Gothic man wrapped in shocking fear is not a pretty sight, she decided, positioning the pillow beneath her thighs and wishing she had trapped Wyatt there, instead. She clenched her legs, squashing the pillows.... If she had him in her clutches now, she'd make him pay for all those "I love you's."

She closed her eyes and mashed the pillows with all her strength. She'd make him pay for tormenting her in that closet with his sisters flitting through the house— Tallulah went still and slowly released the pillows.

She breathed slowly and remembered Wyatt in that dark closet while his sisters fluttered outside.

"Let's get married...."

Tallulah shivered. She'd been married, and it wasn't a picnic.

Fallon stood in the stream wearing Wyatt's waders. She turned to Wyatt, who was sitting on a blanket with Miracle and Leroy, and grinned. "Watch. I can hit that ripple over there."

"Do it, then."

"You think I can't?" she teased with a cheeky grin. "I caught my limit of rainbow yesterday. I've been practicing. Your sisters—my new aunts—coached me."

Wyatt tilted his head to allow Miracle to place a flower over his ear. Leroy, sprawled on the blanket beside them, ate a flower tucked into his harness. He grinned up at Wyatt, realizing that he had an invitation for the night at Fallon's and Wyatt would be watching "Miss Swine" alone in the camper.

Tallulah was sending big "leave me alone, you jerk" signals and Wyatt had decided he would stay away until he came up with a plan she couldn't resist—

Miracle yawned prettily, sought her worn satin blanket and curled into Wyatt's lap. He rocked her and watched his daughter stand on the bank, looking like the long-legged image of his mother.

"I haven't ever felt so good," Fallon was saying as she cast. "Free, you know? Like I'm home with my family around me…. I know it's ridiculous, but that's how I feel."

"Your family is around you," Wyatt offered slowly, watching her.

"Feels that way. Someday I'm going to track down whoever left me that money and thank them until I'm blue in the face and dry in the throat. Maybe kiss a foot or two along the way. Living here, working for Tallulah, having her for my friend—well, more than that—she's really closer. She stayed at my place when I first arrived—I was so scared then—living out of a suitcase…hadn't a clue about how to put a house together. She bullied people into helping me—I know she did, and gradually the house became my first home. Her dad decided he'd clean out his old appliances about then and, boy—"

Fallon cast again and Wyatt studied the clean line of her young profile. "Mr. Michaelson is a great dad. He's there if she needs him, but lets her have her own life. They're a close family."

Wyatt swallowed and tucked his nose into Miracle's curls, letting the childish scents ease the ache in his heart. Tallulah could be sheltering another of his children in her body and he hadn't yet settled his problems with his first daughter.

The last of July shimmered on the leaves of the aspens, as a new insect hatch swirled over the clear stream. Wyatt held

Miracle close to give him strength and said, "Fallon, I want to talk with you."

"Yeah, sure. My arm is giving out anyway," she said with a grin, and waded to the bank.

She stripped off the waders and looked so healthy and happy that Wyatt's heart lurched.

"Sit down," Wyatt offered. "You may have to shove Leroy aside."

An old friend, Leroy eyed Wyatt and grunted his understanding as he eased to the far side of the blanket.

Fallon sprawled on the blanket, her long legs in front of her. "Nice day," she murmured, scanning the sunlight shafting down through the pines. She gazed at him and Wyatt studied her light tan, reminded of her haunted eyes and pale skin when he'd first seen her.

"You love Tallulah, don't you?" Fallon asked gently, then smiled. "She's been nettled something fierce this past week and you've been looking like death warmed over. Well, not quite that bad, but real gloomy—like you've been prowling around mysterious castles or moors or something. Want me to listen? I've been watching Tallulah quite a bit, and I've learned a few things about matchmaking. She's a champion matchmaker, you know. I'm learning from her, and you guys are a match if I ever saw one."

"Fallon, Tallulah and I are moving through difficult stages, but we're clearing out a lot of unnecessary baggage along the way. What I want to talk about is you and me—"

Fallon's expression stilled as though a mask had covered her young face. "What?"

"If you think of my sisters as your aunts, then you might think of me as your father. What do you think?"

She grinned immediately, her eyes sparkling with joy. "You're kidding! Really? Gosh, Wyatt, you're such a neat guy. I've never called anyone 'Dad' before. Really?"

"I'd like that, Fallon," Wyatt said gently. He inhaled slowly before he continued. "Because you see, I really am

your father and Miracle's grandfather. You are Fallon
Louise Remington, born at the Little Sweet Hospital at 3:31
in the morning. You had a triangular birthmark on your
right backside."

"No way," she answered flatly, her eyes wary as they
studied him carefully. Then her eyes widened. "No way,"
she repeated, drawing a sleeping Miracle from him and into
her arms.

The protective move, sheltering her daughter against her,
was poignant.

Wyatt closed his eyes, trying to dim the pain racing
through him. "I never hurt your mother, Fallon. Never
touched her in any way but the way a man touches a woman
he loves. I did love her then."

Fallon held Miracle tight against her, and the sleeping
child protested slightly. "Mom said you hurt her. That she
was afraid you'd find us and then you'd—"

Wyatt took a deep breath and prayed she'd believe him.
That she'd know the truth by looking at him and following
the gentle, warm bond that had grown between them. "Our
feelings for each other changed. Your mother was frightened my clan would have taken you away. She swore that
you'd never see them or me and that you'd never want to.
She changed both your names to Smith—tracing a Smith
across Europe and the United States is like finding the traditional needle in a haystack."

"But you found us."

"It wasn't easy." He paused and nudged her foot with his
toe. "What do you think, Fallon?"

Fallon looked away to a big gold leaf caught by the swirling water. She edged her foot away from Wyatt's. "I think
you planned this. I think somehow you found us—me and
Miracle—and that you planned how we would live here in
Elegance."

"Where you would be safe," Wyatt added gently, aching
to fold her into his arms.

"Safe," she repeated dully as the leaf sank from sight.

Wyatt carefully took a folded paper from his wallet and eased it open. "This is a copy of your birth certificate, Fallon. I've followed you across Europe, Canada and just about everywhere in the United States. I was just a step behind all the time and once—"

He omitted the time his ex-wife had set thugs on him, telling them she feared for her life. His three months in the hospital had allowed her to cover her trail very well—for a time. He'd served time in jails for harassment, while she skipped away with Fallon—

Fallon took the paper and scanned it quickly, her expression taut. "So what?"

"Think about it," Wyatt offered slowly, his heart thudding heavily within his chest as Fallon rose to her feet and carried Miracle to his pickup.

When they parked at the small house he'd purchased for her, Fallon spoke again tightly. "Thanks for the ride."

Thanks... but no thanks for the years wasted....

Wyatt forced himself to place the pickup in gear and move away from her house.

She'd led a lifetime of running.... Would she run now? Would she believe him?

Then there was Tallulah, who was possibly carrying his baby. *Would she want a child now? Would she want the shape of her life changed?* The fear of not raising another child who was his rammed through Wyatt.

Another, darker fear, that of losing Tallulah when they had just begun, stilled his heart. He clenched his fingers, then released them from the steering wheel; he listened to the beating of his pulse and knew that he needed Tallulah to be whole to live again—

A sour taste rose in his mouth. He was wrong to offer her marriage so soon and in that casual way, to ask if she wanted to start a family. He'd frightened her badly.

He stared sightlessly at the gray pavement beneath his headlights. He saw Tallulah's pale, vulnerable face as she had asked him about making a baby—

"I love you. Making a baby with you would be—"

He could have unrolled his love for Tallulah, told her how happy she had made him—anything. But he hadn't.

Wyatt almost pulled the truck to the side of the road and spilled his fears upon the rocks.

Tallulah looked at Wyatt's broad back as he sat on the café stool. She gripped Sam Payton's plate of fresh-broiled trout with lemon tighter. Shrouded in his orphan-pup look, Wyatt was almost irresistible.... Almost.

She ached to press her chest against Wyatt. To rest against him and listen to his soft drawl telling her everything would be perfect.

Deep within her, her body quivered and tightened.

"I want you.... I love you...."

The urge to lay him out on the counter and have him à la deluxe startled her.

Thirty-eight was a fine time to find that she was highly sexually charged. *And that she loved a man who was frightened of having his swimmers put to the test....*

She'd had enough experience with one man on that account.

Wyatt Remington, Mr. W. R. Lures of the wary glances, had no need to fear.

Tallulah glanced at her various exes, who were looking at her with concern. Their wives and girlfriends patted her hand and whispered their sympathies. Norm hovered in the cook's window, peering out worriedly.

Fallon whooshed by, appearing grim as she delivered the Joneses sundaes with nuts on top. She shot a look at Wyatt that scalded Tallulah, who was in his vicinity.

Tallulah served the broiled trout, poured extra ice water and warmed up empty coffee cups with more brew. In the meantime she also studied Wyatt's grim face and Fallon's brittle expression.

After ignoring Wyatt for a week, the first week of August seemed like a fine time to clear the air—at least between Wyatt and his daughter.

"I feel like my skin is too tight and all my body parts are cheering, 'Wyatt...Wyatt...we want Wyatt....'" Tallulah muttered. She grabbed a slice of blackberry pie and slid the plate in front of Wyatt, who had just finished his first slice. He deserved a second slice, since Jack hadn't rated a cheer of any kind from her heart or her body.

Wyatt glanced up at her, his eyes shadowy and his mouth grim. "You told Fallon, didn't you? You look like death warmed over," she said without kindness, though her heart was bleeding for his pain.

When he nodded slowly, Tallulah inhaled. "It didn't go well, did it?"

"We'll work it out," Wyatt said carefully. He eyed the second slice of pie, then her. She noted a wary fear scooting through his dark eyes as he asked, "How are you feeling?"

She glared at him—the father of her baby, who was afraid of real commitment when actually faced with it. Talk about swimmers was all right, but now that they'd actually done their job, Wyatt was having second thoughts.... Well, he wouldn't have to commit, would he?

She'd failed at marriage once, so Mr. W. R. Lures was safe from her clutches. Though she hadn't tried motherhood yet, she wouldn't fail that course.

If she was blessed and a child grew within her, she'd love it enough for two parents, and shelter and nurture and protect—

Still, she wanted him to be happy and his quest for Fallon to end as it should. "What's it to you?" she asked tightly. "Come to my house for supper tonight. We'll work this out. You and Fallon and Miracle and—"

Tallulah swallowed, trying not to think of cooking dinner and the way the scents unsettled her stomach. She glanced at the plate of over-easy eggs Norm had just placed under the warming light. "I'll think of something to cook. Norm can fix carryout."

"I'll cook." Wyatt wrapped his fingers around her wrist, his thumb stroking the sensitive skin over her rapidly beating pulse. "I don't suppose you and I could get out of here and settle what's between us now," he asked, then leaned across to kiss her in a way that was sweeter than July's blackberry pie.

When she slowly opened her eyes—drifting back into reality—Wyatt was standing near her, smelling so good and looking so fine—

"Dance?" he asked huskily as one of the exes pushed a quarter into the machine.

"You're fast," Tallulah muttered a few seconds later as Wyatt placed her arms around his shoulders and drew her close to him. She realized that he had taken away her glasses and they lay on the counter. He folded her gently against him as though he was gathering her to his heart to stay.

"I love you, Tallulah Jane. We'll get through this," he murmured close to her ear.

When her tears began, Wyatt tucked her face into the curve of his throat. "You stay put, Tallulah. You're where you should be," he whispered, stroking her back.

"Oh, you poor man," she almost wailed against his warm skin.

He tensed. "What do you mean?"

"It's all so sad," she managed unevenly, holding him tightly and wishing she could protect him from more pain. She gripped his T-shirt in her fists—

"I'm not looking for sympathy," Wyatt said grimly after a moment.

She shivered again as a feeling passed between them that had nothing to do with sympathy and everything to do with heat and storms and heaven. Wyatt looked as though in another second he would swoop her up and carry her off....

His gaze slid down to her chest and his eyes darkened; a flush rose up his cheeks as he met her widened eyes. "It's more than wanting," he said unevenly. His jaw moved as though he was determined to have his say, then he continued firmly. "It's a lifetime loving feeling."

"I..." She cleared her tight throat. "I think I'd better go make some french-fried onion rings," she said a little too loudly, grabbed her glasses and pushed them on her nose.

"Have mercy," the customers answered in unison.

"Dad," Fallon stated flatly, coldly, as she handed the platter of fettuccine Alfredo to Wyatt. The girl leveled her gaze at Tallulah. "We look alike, don't we?" she demanded of Tallulah in that same, flat tone.

Fallon passed the tossed salad to Tallulah. "Miracle looks just like me and I look like my new aunts and my new dad, isn't that right...*Dad?*" she said tightly, bitterly.

"Paw-paw," Miracle said brightly, grinning at Wyatt with her small, bright, perfect baby teeth. She squirmed on the high chair and held up a pitless olive on her small finger.

Fallon watched her daughter and shivered, tears coming to her eyes. "It's too much," she muttered, her lips trembling.

Tallulah shot a "let me handle this" look at Wyatt, who realized belatedly that his expression must have revealed his helpless feelings. She placed another olive on Miracle's chubby finger, then put her hand on Fallon's thin shoulder. "He loves you. Look at him. He's bleeding inside, aching for you."

Wyatt inhaled sharply. "I can manage this, Tallulah."

"No, you can't," she returned evenly. "You've got that all-drawn-in look, just like you're waiting for someone to kick you."

Wyatt ran his fingers through his hair and glanced from Fallon's young tense face to Tallulah's concerned one. Battling two females on two separate issues at once wasn't that easy. He didn't want Tallulah's sympathy; he wanted the emotions that ran between them to be strong and unclouded. "I don't need you to protect me, Tallulah. I am not one of your buddies or one of your causes."

Undaunted by his ominous tone, she returned his dark look. "Don't you bring my exes into this. I wouldn't have you for a cause if you were offered to me on a platter. Trust me...you will never rate with my exes," she finished heatedly.

"Well, hallelujah," Wyatt snapped, and threw his napkin on the table. Right now, balancing his emotions for two women, trying to hold his own—he suddenly realized he was speaking aloud.... "I'd really appreciate getting my hands on one of the backup boys right now. I'd like to relieve a bit of frustration."

"Don't you touch a one of them, Wyatt Sebastian Remington," she ordered tightly. "They are sweet—"

"And I'm not?" he demanded. "Try getting along with a red-haired whirlwind who is the town busybody...and who should pay more attention to her own love life—which we have well and good, Tallulah dear. I have passed my matchmaking lessons and you'd better take care, because I am truly not that son of a buck you married the first time."

Her eyes widened. "Oh! Oh!"

Fallon patted her eyes with her cloth napkin, then sent Wyatt a searching look. He unlocked his glare from Tallulah's and braced himself for whatever his daughter was about to say—

"I'm not much to be proud of.... From your sisters...ah...my aunts, I guess the Remington family must be pretty upstanding, huh? Classy people? Well, I'm not. I can't even read...isn't that a hoot? When Miracle hands me a children's book, I don't read it—I fake it. I don't know why it matters much now if *I am your daughter.*"

Wyatt ached for Fallon. "It matters, honey. You're a part of me, my blood, my baby girl. It matters."

"Fallon, there are adult classes forming now—" Tallulah began, and stopped when she saw that Wyatt and his daughter were locked in a separate, dark, bristling arena. Wyatt felt all of his years, his face taut with the tension swirling around the room.

"I wanted you every minute," Wyatt said huskily, aching to draw Fallon against him. He also thought of how he wanted the child that Tallulah might be carrying, and hoped that what ran between them was true enough to survive. To hold a second child in his arms would be heaven. "You're a part of me, my deepest, best part. The part of me that will go on forever, and I'll be proud knowing that."

"Sure. Uh-huh. Right. Why weren't you here?" Fallon hurled the words at him, her face white and her thin body shaking. "Do you know how scared I was coming on the bus with Miracle? I've never lived in a real house before, always apartments. A house squeaks as it settles for the night, do you know that?" she demanded shakily, tears running down her cheeks. "Why weren't you here?"

Wyatt swallowed heavily, his face pale beneath his tan. "I was on that bus from Chicago," he admitted slowly. "I knew you were afraid to fly. I watched you find the house and go into it. I knew you'd be safe then."

Her eyes widened and she stood to hurriedly take Miracle from the high chair. Miracle, sensing the emotions swirling over her head, had begun to look fearful. "Mama?"

"You mean you pulled this cloak-and-dagger stuff, tracked me across the country and didn't have the nerve to introduce yourself?" Fallon said shakily. "When did you find us?"

Wyatt knew his agony was written in his expression. Fallon gripped Miracle tighter and the child's bottom lip began to pucker. Tallulah reached to hold her chubby hand and kissed her cheek.

Wyatt hesitated; he didn't want to tell Fallon that he'd seen her at her lowest—

Tallulah spoke gently. "Fallon, he's found you and he's arranged to keep you and your baby safe."

He gave a silent thankful prayer for Tallulah's gentle intrusion—

"Safe!" Fallon almost spit the word, tears streaming down her cheeks. She hurriedly stuffed Miracle into her light jacket. "I want to go home. Tallulah, you brought me. Will you take us home now?"

Wyatt rose slowly, every one of his years weighting his shoulders. "Tallulah has had a hard day, Fallon. I'll take you home."

Fallon balanced Miracle on her hip. She studied Tallulah's face, and Wyatt's dark gaze followed. He frowned and pushed her gently down into the chair. "Stay put."

He looked at Fallon, his expression strained. He realized that he had been holding Tallulah's shoulder, and forced his fingers away. This was his battle and he would fight it alone. "I knew how you thought of me. I found out from the people who knew you and your mother. I never hurt her…and I didn't think I would get a good reception from you. I decided to take it slow.… The other thing I knew was that you were my daughter and you had grown into a beautiful, loving person despite being dragged through a hard life. I knew you would protect Miracle. I'm asking you to forgive me—"

"Forgive?" Fallon erupted. "A lifetime of thinking— Do you have any idea of how scared I was as a kid—left alone for days in apartments while Mom went off—"

Wyatt looked as though she had just slapped him. He swallowed slowly, his lips tightening. "You're tired. Can I take you home?"

Leroy came to stand against Wyatt's leg. He leaned gently against his master, gazed up at Fallon with beady eyes and began a series of sympathetic grunts. Despite her raw emotions, Fallon glanced down. With tears running down her eyes, she asked, "What kind of a dad has a pig for a pet?"

Tallulah reached to place her arm around Fallon's thin waist. She rocked her slightly and Fallon's hand gripped hers for an instant, then slid away.

"Pig!" Miracle exclaimed happily, sensing that the tension had lightened. "Want pig." She almost dived out of her mother's arms, and Fallon lowered her. Miracle sat on the floor and wrapped her arms around Leroy's neck. "Pretty pig," she crooned.

Fallon shifted restlessly, looking very young in her ruffled blouse and tight jeans. "I guess we'll take Leroy for the night as we had planned," she said reluctantly. Then she turned to Wyatt. "You can take us home, but I don't want to talk.... Just don't you say anything bad about my mother," she ordered tightly.

"No," he promised softly, and forgave Michelle's twisted mind. She had given him Fallon, a perfect gift. "I won't."

Wyatt sat on Tallulah's front porch, letting the lonely night gently wrap around him. Fallon had been tense, moving quickly out of his pickup and into her house. He recognized the pain, the need to be alone and lick wounds that were so deep she feared sharing them with others.

He scanned the stars overhead and thought how many miles, how many countries and how many nights he'd sat alone, wishing for his daughter—

If she ran now— He pushed back that churning, lashing fear and inhaled deeply. He caught the scent of batter-fried onions. Wyatt smiled slightly. "Nice night, isn't it, Tallulah?"

She moved out of the shadows to his side and Wyatt found her hand to help her down onto the step beside him.

He placed his arm around her and drew her close. "You've been making onion rings?"

She sniffed. "Just a few. They're hot. Do you want some?"

Wyatt had eaten enough onion rings to last him a lifetime. "Not right now."

He nuzzled her hair and let the warmth of her ease his aching heart. "You're a softhearted woman, Tallulah Jane. You're worried about Fallon and Miracle and me, aren't you?"

She placed her head on his shoulder. "Someone has to. Poor Fallon...all alone in those apartments, a frightened child."

When she sniffed again, Wyatt lifted her face to scan her teary eyes. "And who worries about you, Little Miss Worrywart?"

He carefully lifted her onto his lap and adjusted the worn chenille robe around her legs against the evening chill. "Have you come out here in the night to vamp me?" he whispered into her soft hair.

"Huh!" she said flatly, and placed her hand over Wyatt's as he smoothed her stomach.

Wyatt allowed the tenderness and the warmth he felt for this special woman to seep through him. He nuzzled her damp cheek. "Have you come to tell me that you love me and want me and can't live without me? That if you can't have me, you'll cook onion rings from dawn to dusk every day of the rest of your life?"

"Huh!" she repeated in that same scornful, flat tone. "I used onion-ring therapy before I ever met you."

"Hmm, then you might want to tell me about your ex-boyfriends and how you purely miss kissing this one and living with that one—"

Tallulah's head came up and Wyatt kissed away a strand of her silky hair. She glared at him in the moonlight. "I have never lived with a man other than my ex-husband."

"Uh-huh. Wasn't much fun, was it?"

She looked at him darkly. "I'm not talking about him."

"Then tell me how you felt about your string of ex's. Did you love every one?"

Tallulah inhaled impatiently. "You know very well that you are the only man to—to..." She cleared her throat before continuing. "To share my bed. I liked keeping the guys safe and matching them to the right woman. There was never anything...very warm in my relationships—"

"You are one loving woman, Tallulah," Wyatt drawled in his soft, deep, magnolia-drenched voice.

She scowled up at him. "Stop prowling around in what happened between my ex's and myself. None of them seemed highly sexed, so it really wasn't a problem."

"Ah! Sex wasn't a problem," he said with delight. "I'm the only man to partake of your flaming passion—so that must mean that I'm a step ahead of the backup boys."

"I'm not a casual person, Wyatt," she stated primly, covering her bare knee with the edge of her robe. "We discussed that before we... We're both monogamous."

Wyatt let the rich warmth of pleasure slide over him. "Seems to me like monogamous people should keep each other, don't you think? Sort of an 'I've got you,' dibs thing?"

When Tallulah clamped her lips against uttering the fiery retort he read in her eyes, Wyatt kissed the tip of her nose and lingered over her lips. "Tell me how they kissed...light, like this—" He brushed a kiss over her lips.

"Or like forever," he murmured, realizing that this one woman held his heart.

Tallulah reached to slide her fingers through his hair and tug him closer. To Wyatt, her warmth was like a homecoming, and he treated her very gently, gathering her closer. He placed his hand upon her breast, noted the changed, taut fullness, and was filled with the miracle of having a child with her.

"I love you, Tallulah Jane," Wyatt said softly, meaning it and praying that she did care for him in some special way.

Tallulah scanned his face, tracing the lines and the shape of his eyes, his cheeks and his lips. She stroked the evening stubble with her palm, and Wyatt kissed her hand as it passed. "Give Fallon time," she whispered, smoothing his hair back over his ear. "She'll come around."

He brushed away a strand of hair from her cheek and pain ripped through him again. He found that he was sharing his fears aloud. "I am praying that she doesn't run."

"Fallon is a smart girl. She's a mother and knows where her child is safe. I don't think she'll leave us," Tallulah stated after a moment.

Then she kissed him lightly. "I think you had better come inside, Wyatt," she whispered. "Old Mrs. Jones across the street has binoculars that she doesn't use on bird-watching."

"You are a dangerous woman, Miss Tallulah," Wyatt murmured as he stood slowly, lifting her with him. "I truly fear for my well-being. However, I shall accept your kind invitation and leave my safety to your care."

Her husky, mysterious laughter had everything to do with life and laughter and nothing to do with his safety or the gloomy past.

Nine

"**D**ad?" Fallon called from downstairs.

Tallulah blinked against the morning sunshine. Her bedside clock read seven o'clock. She should have been pouring second cups of coffee at the café by this hour....

Wyatt's large, warm hand spanned her stomach, caressing her; he was making awakening, hungry, sensual noises.

"Dad? Tallulah, I see Dad's pickup out front. Is he here?" Fallon called, and the clatter of Leroy's hooves echoed from the living room.

"Paw-paw?" Miracle called.

Leroy squealed and grunted, running through the house.

"Mmm," Wyatt murmured drowsily beside Tallulah as his hand moved lower.

Tallulah scowled at the bouquet of flowers on her dresser. She had pitted her passions against Wyatt's and found that he had withstood the test several times during the night. Wyatt had confirmed to her that she was a desirable, passionate woman. That when their hearts were racing together and Wyatt was whispering in her ear, telling her of his love—

He had touched her soul and she loved him for who he was, a sweet, gentle man and a rogue doing his best for his loved ones.... That was why she could give her body to him without restraint—because of who he was inside, the beauty of his heart and soul.

She studied a tiny purple wildflower, picked by Miracle the day before, and knew that she loved Wyatt deeply.

The wildflower quivered in the sunlight as Tallulah swallowed and blinked.

"I want you.... I love you...."

Tallulah placed her hand over her heart. She had tried marriage and had failed miserably. Wyatt's sense of nobility would demand that he do the honorable act and marry her to give his child the Remington name. Tallulah's throat tightened and she swallowed her fear heavily. She placed her hand over Wyatt's foraging one and lifted it away.

"Wyatt, wake up," Tallulah muttered, rummaging for her T-shirt. She found it lodged beneath Wyatt's stomach and tugged it away. She jammed her arms through it and tried to squirm her legs free of his anchoring thigh.

His hand slid up under the shirt to find her breast and caress it gently. He opened one eye and murmured in his deepest, most Southern tones, "I feel like I've been delightfully mashed and zapped. I could use another mashing, Tallulah-honey. I love listening to your pretty little screams of delight."

She stared down at him. "I do not scream, Wyatt Sebastian Remington."

His hand roamed her thigh. "Do, too. Prettiest little screams...like you're giving your soul and your love to me."

The tiny purple wildflower quivered in the slight breeze from the open window. Wyatt's fingers tightened ever so much on her thigh—a gentle claiming as he waited for her to speak. Then he demanded huskily, unevenly, "Just what do you think all this is about?"

Tallulah sensed that Wyatt was asking for the commitment that she didn't want to give—not just yet.

She loved him.

Her heart thudded loudly in her chest.... She caught the pain, quickly concealed, shafting through Wyatt's dark eyes.

Tallulah breathed heavily, stunned by the sight of Wyatt's bare backside; it gleamed under the window's sunlight. "You're not wearing a stitch," she muttered, jerking up the covers.

Wyatt flipped over and dragged her beneath the covers. "Gotcha," he said before kissing her. In the next instant he was burrowing under her shirt, nuzzling her navel.

"Fallon and Miracle are here," she whispered unevenly under the covers. She held his head still and tried not to giggle. "It's seven o'clock and I should be down at the Tall Order—"

"Paw-paw?" Miracle's childish voice was saying, her footsteps sounding on the stairs.

Leroy oinked angrily, a sound he made because he couldn't climb the stairs with Fallon. "Miracle, how many times have I told you not to— Leroy, stop that. You'll have to wait until we come down. There is not a ramp long enough to reach up there," Fallon ordered, then called, "Dad?"

Miracle giggled as she came into the room and patted Tallulah's head, then Wyatt's beneath the covers. "Got you!" she exclaimed with delight.

In the shadows of the covers, Wyatt grinned at Tallulah. He looked rakish and playful as he repeated, "Got you."

Tallulah scowled back at him and cleared her throat. "Ah...we'll be right out, Fallon."

But Wyatt was dragging her upward, plumping the pillows behind them and drawing the covers up to his waist.

His arm gripped Tallulah's waist. He brushed away a strand of hair from her hot cheek.

"Say something, Wyatt," she whispered desperately. "You know how this must look."

Wyatt's mouth moved and his eyes crinkled at the corners as he fought a grin. Tallulah knew that it looked just like what it was—the morning after his staying in her bed.

"Wyatt!" Tallulah begged. "Think of something."

"Okay." Then he turned to his daughter, who lingered in the doorway. "You called me 'Dad,' Fallon," he stated quietly. "Thank you."

She shrugged self-consciously. "Sure. No big deal."

Tallulah had been hoping for a reasonable presentation of Wyatt in her bed, but the new twist fascinated her.

"It is to me," Wyatt said softly as he helped Miracle climb up next to him.

Tallulah held very still, sensing that Wyatt wanted her to remain near him. Her mind distantly noted that it was a strange, new event to be lying next to a man in a room filled with people. She locked her fingers on his wrist, taking safety in his strength.

Fallon hesitantly came farther inside the room, rubbing the toe of her jogger against the braided rug. "I thought you guys might want to go fishing...."

"I tired," Miracle announced, snuggling down between Tallulah and Wyatt.

"She had a bad night," Fallon explained with a tired sigh as her daughter's eyes closed. "She worries when she sees me cry."

Wyatt frowned, his expression grim. "We'll get past this, Fallon. I understand how you feel. It is a big adjustment. We can work out our problems."

The distance between Wyatt and his daughter was closing, Tallulah thought as she yawned. She snuggled Miracle close and found that Wyatt's fingers caressing her nape had made her drowsy. "I'll keep her," she said with a yawn, and curled herself around the little girl. "Go fishing. Just don't catch my big one.... Uh, call Norm for me?"

The second week of August, Wyatt inhaled the fresh morning air and swallowed slowly. He cast, then rubbed his unsettled stomach. Dealing with two very different women would make any man uneasy.

Taking Tallulah's place in the morning—baking pies and serving breakfasts with Fallon—had settled Wyatt's unstable life with Tallulah. She resented sleeping late and napping in the afternoon. She was wary, quirky, unhappy and skitterish, and that was when she wasn't passionate, delighted with life and wanting to play volleyball and softball. She terrified Norm, her father and the exes, and cried when Wyatt gave her another red-rose bouquet. He suspected her ex-husband had lacked finer points and damned him for his cruelty to Tallulah.

Tension in Elegance was rising like a hungry trout swirling in the bottom waters until deciding to surface—

This morning, Norm had insisted Wyatt go fishing, as he was looking "peaked and a little winded."

Fallon dealt with her new knowledge in traditional Remington methodical style. She waded through the years at her own pace, asking Wyatt questions when they occurred to her. She had lost the purplish shadows beneath her eyes and her laughter came more easily. Then there were times when she just stared into space, and he knew that she was thinking of her mother. Discovering her life had been a lie hadn't been easy, but Fallon had risen to the challenge and was facing the damage her mother had done.

Her delight in the lure he had created for her, a quivering bright yellow affair with dark fur, had warmed him.

Tallulah had sobbed openly, allowing Wyatt to hold her on his lap and cuddle her.

Wyatt frowned at the brown trout lurching out of the stream's depths to leap at the Tallulah.

At the moment, cuddling Tallulah was a delicate matter. She could erupt into passion at one touch....

Wyatt smiled slowly, allowing the trout's open mouth to come within a fraction of an inch to the Tallulah. He was certain that she had never released the passion within her to another man. "Stubborn woman," he murmured gently, playing the lure.

He'd picked a strong woman. Tallulah might release her passion behind the bedroom door, but she was wounded by love and wary of committing herself to him. Fighter that she was, working out her problems with love, she wouldn't have much longer before the baby was no longer a secret.

Their nights in her tiny, ruffled, creaking bed scorched the sheets.

Tallulah slept a great deal and flushed when Wyatt mentioned the fact and how she should see a doctor about her upset stomach.

Wyatt swallowed heavily; he rubbed his stomach and decided that perhaps he should stop eating huge breakfasts until Tallulah's emotions settled down a bit. He closed his eyes when he remembered his morning eggs shining up at him.

He swallowed again, dismissing the scent of onions, which was now saturating every corner of his life.

A new baby and his daughter and granddaughter— Wyatt grinned, then realized that his emotions were as unstable as Tallulah's.

He wanted her to come to him because she wanted to, not because they had created a tiny miracle between them. He envisioned a little Tallulah zipping through the house and nurturing her friends.

Wyatt grinned hugely. Another baby... another baby to hold against him and cuddle. Another baby to bring into his growing family, to share the love that grew daily between Fallon and him.

He remembered the teddy bear in the dry-goods store and decided to give it to Tallulah—

In the middle of the café's midmorning coffee hour, Tallulah looked at the large fuzzy teddy bear in her hands and at Miracle's grin as she held her new baby doll. Seated on Wyatt's shoulders, the little girl giggled. Fallon hugged the huge panda that Wyatt had just given her and stood on tiptoe to kiss his cheek. When he wrapped his arm around her shoulders, Fallon tensed, then slowly slid her arm around him.

The three of them stood together in the Tall Order—father, daughter and granddaughter—looking goofy and dear with great big grins and waiting for her to say something. They looked perfect as Elvis sang "Love Me Tender" in the background.

This was her baby's family—the Remingtons, lately from the Georgia Remingtons. Her heart leaped and twisted and burst with joy.

Her fingers gripped the counter and she heard herself announcing baldly, "Wyatt, I am carrying your child."

The midmorning coffee customers turned to stare at her. Tex, always taking his paramedic duties seriously, pulled the electric cord on the jukebox.

Norm, chewing on his toothpick, came to stand at the counter beside Tallulah.

Her fingertips ached from gripping the counter.

Wyatt slowly handed Miracle to Fallon, who was looking from Tallulah to Wyatt anxiously. He inhaled, and shot a dark glance around at the customers, who were staring openly. His gaze met Tex's and the paramedic shook his head sadly.

Wyatt inhaled again, then walked slowly to Tallulah. He watched her intently. She shifted her weight from one leg to the other. Norm switched his toothpick to the other side of his mouth and stepped back.

Her announcement quivered in the still air as Wyatt continued to loom over her. "You picked a fine time, Tallulah Jane."

She glanced at the concerned expressions around the room, her flush slowly creeping up her throat to her cheeks. "Ah...Wyatt...ah...you know, you have been emotional lately."

His forefinger thrust gently against her chest; he refused to be distracted by her accusation. "I am not making this easy," he said. "I won't ask you again.... I want you to come with me now. We have a deep and genuine need to discuss matters between us in a private, unobserved manner," he said in very formal, Southern-male tone.

She clung to the counter. He was asking her to leave one life and begin anew with him.

To forget her pain and her past and walk into the future—

She'd given everything once to Jack and had it slashed apart— Fear ran through her like live, cold, silvery snakes.

She shivered, lashed by her fears and her need to have Wyatt hold her. Above her, he looked grim and unrelenting.

He'd left the choice to her.

She foundered, her mind awash with questions and wanting to tell Wyatt that she needed him, that she felt her life was just starting—

Pain ran through his face, sharpening the lines and darkening his eyes before Wyatt stilled his expression.

"Remember this, Tallulah Jane." Wyatt's forefinger jabbed gently into her chest. "Because whatever happens, this is how it is."

Then he drew her around the corner of the counter, looked down her body and fitted his hand over her stomach. "This is my child, Tallulah, and I claim it as mine. I'll love our baby and tend it and do what must be done. But from you, I'll be wanting something else."

Then he bent her over his arm and kissed her breathless. She clung to his shoulders, forgot the customers were watching and gave him her heart.

When Tallulah recovered, she blinked up at Norm's grizzled frown. The toothpick switched back and forth in his leathery lips as he shook his head. "Girl, you need lessons," he muttered as he watched Wyatt lift Leroy into the passenger side of his truck and drive away.

Tallulah licked her sensitive lips, tasted Wyatt's stunning kiss and glanced at Tex, who was shaking his head sadly as he talked to the Browns. Norm peered through the cook's window. "Get in here. You're embarrassing me."

Tallulah's legs felt rubbery as she entered the kitchen. Norm looked at her as though she'd committed a crime. "I want this baby," she stated. "I'm having Wyatt's baby—or I think I am—so don't start on me about anything else."

"You can't just dish that out on a platter to a man in front of everybody." Norm shut the cook's window, which signified to all those in the restaurant that they would wait until he was ready. He crossed his arms. "Look, kid. Wyatt has been feeling, well . . . sensitive. He's a little pale around the gills sometimes, you know. Tension does that to a man—well . . ."

Norm shifted his weight uneasily and looked away. "Well, I suppose there is other things if a guy isn't sleeping regular. . . . I mean, if I guy doesn't get his regular eight—"

"I love him," she said. "That's how it is."

Norm closed his eyes, then opened them as he looked up for heavenly guidance. "A guy needs romance . . . kisses . . . and most of all being alone with his gal when she gives him news like that. Tallulah, you lack technique. Get some," he said, before jerking open the cook's window. "And get some fluffy female slithery stuff to wear once in a while. . . . And stop cooking onions. A guy needs a drift of eau de woman once in a while."

Fallon came through the kitchen doors and put her arm around Tallulah's shoulders. "Dad is happy about the baby. So am I. He's just got his nose out of joint for some reason.... Ah, maybe you should have told him in private—"

Tex pushed through the doors, crossed his arms over his massive chest and frowned at Tallulah. "Stretch, you can't just flop something like that out in public. It's a candles thing."

Tallulah knew her reputation as a matchmaker and teacher of romance was in the proverbial toilet.

She also knew the next move was hers.

"This is going to be real good," Tex noted softly.

Norm nodded sagely. "Real good."

"You can forget about volleyball and softball, Stretch. Once I tell your exes, you won't be allowed to play. So I guess you'd better try upping your scores in romance, huh?" Tex asked.

That night, Tallulah sat on the floor with her arm around Leroy; her father sat in his favorite overstuffed chair. She grabbed a pillow and hugged it with her free arm. How was she supposed to know that pregnancy could raise a woman's sexual urges?

How was she supposed to know that Wyatt was the only man who made her feel complete, totally desirable, loved and needed?

"I messed up, Dad," she muttered.

"So I heard. Told Wyatt about my supposed coming grandchild just like you were announcing a change in the soup du jour. He loves you, Tallie. But you've got to go a bit here to make up for your flub-up. Now, the ideal thing would have been a nice romantic dinner, give the guy a chance to adjust to the situation, then set the hook and reel him in."

"Like my big one down at the stream," Tallulah murmured absently, wishing she had waited for a more romantic moment.

Her father laughed outright. "Honey, Wyatt is your big one. I knew it from the moment I saw you two sight down on each other. Smoke came out of your ears and you headed for him like an engine afire. A man like Wyatt is going to react one way—he's a fighter, just like you. But he's real tender now... wary of the hook. You'll have to try different bait," he suggested with a wide grin.

"I thought he should know," Tallulah stated in her defense. "I don't want him obligated to marry me because of our baby."

"I'll just bet he isn't the one that is ring-shy, honey," her father answered softly. "You better think about that."

"He hasn't caught a stringer of fish since he's been here," she said. She smoothed the pillow and wished she were mashing Wyatt's broad, dark, hairy chest against her aching breasts.

"Oh, I'd say he's caught a keeper."

Tallulah gathered Leroy closer and wondered distantly when she had learned to hug and confide in the porker. "'Keep my pig.' That's all he said before he attached his trailer to his pickup and zoomed out of town.... 'Keep my pig.' Dad, that's not a real 'I love you,' now is it?"

"Tallie, you know that he has that sports show in Abstinence, seventy-five miles away. He's got to be there at dawn because they are starting the fishing tournament and he's the main celebrity."

Leroy grunted sympathetically and snuggled closer to Tallulah. He looked at her with lonely beady eyes. "'Keep my pig,'" Tallulah said, brooding, rubbing Leroy's bristly back. "He just stood there on the porch, looking tough and Gothic in his battered leather jacket, jeans and boots. The rain and the mist even swirled around him and lightning lit the rain in his hair. He just loomed over me for a time as though he was waiting for me to do something. Then he handed me Leroy's leash and said, 'Keep my pig.' Dad, that's not really romantic, especially when a woman has just told a man that she is having his baby.''

"Well, I'd say that's the next thing to asking you to take care of his baby and that he'll be back for you. Why don't you just take tomorrow off and drive up to Abstinence, Tallie?''

"Humph. No way. You weren't there this morning, Dad. He said he wouldn't make it easy.'' Tallulah leveled a look at her father. "He's not exactly Mr. Easy anyway.''

"He's had a hard life and you've nicked his pride. The way I see it is that anything worth having is worth the struggle. You've never had to struggle to get a man or to keep him. Are you willing to show Wyatt you care?''

Tallulah stroked Leroy's back and he grinned hopefully up at her. "Wyatt is cute, isn't he, Dad?'' she murmured with a soft smile.

"Uh? Cute? Wyatt?'' Her father stared at her blankly, then he began roaring with laughter.

Wyatt closed his "makings" box and shook his head. When he asked Tallulah to leave the café with him, she'd gripped the counter with both hands. Her knuckles had turned white.

He rubbed his eyes, the gritty feel reminding him of his lack of sleep. At two o'clock in the morning, he had time for five hours of sleep before opening the fishing tournament. He glanced in the camper's small mirror and rubbed his hand across his jaw. The scrape of stubble against his palm suited his dark mood. With shadows lurking around his eyes and his hair standing out from the many times he'd run his fingers through it, he did look like a "Gothic guy.''

The dim light caught the gray in his hair and Wyatt's lips tightened, the lines in his face deepening. "An *old* Gothic guy,'' he muttered as a knock sounded on his door.

"Wyatt, are you in there?" Tallulah called softly.

He jerked open the screen door, opened the door itself too quickly, and watched Tallulah dance backward to avoid getting hit. "What are you doing here?" he asked, taking in the black dress that clung to her curves. He looked down to the short hemline, which exposed a length of long legs.

Her head went back. Light from the electric pole lamp over the camper trailer park caught the rain glistening on her hair. Tallulah hitched the strap over her shoulder higher and gripped the big black bag at her side. The movement raised her breasts in the low-cut bodice and the rain sparkled on her skin.

"What are you doing dressed like that? Where's your raincoat?" Wyatt demanded as he reached out to help her into the camper.

He grabbed a towel and started patting her face and her bodice dry. He bent, slid off her heels and propped her foot on his thigh as he dried her skin. When he stood, he belatedly noticed she was wearing hose. "You'll catch cold."

"Are you or are you not glad to see me, Wyatt?" she demanded tautly as she dropped her bag to the floor.

The weight hurt his bare feet, but Wyatt was too deep in his mood to care. "I've changed my mind," he stated, moving the bag aside with his foot. "Commitment won't do. I'm wanting more."

She studied him and eased back a strand of hair from his brow. He kissed her hand as it passed and noted that Tallulah clasped it tight with her other hand. "What do you want from me?" she asked unevenly. "What's the bottom line? What are the rules?"

Wyatt weighed his words. He'd sprung marriage and swimmers on her too soon. She was wary now, but she had come to him. "I can't let you have me too easy," he heard himself saying. "We have a baby between us and I want him or her to know that I can hold my own with his red-haired whirlwind of a mother. There's that to consider and there's more, too. Like a balance between us."

He was gambling now, his heart racing with fear that she would leave. "I want to know for certain that you never think of me as you think of your ex-husband. That you know I'll never hurt you."

He swallowed the tightness in his throat. "I need to know that you don't feel pushed into a corner—that you feel you have to care for me because you're carrying my baby."

If she left him now, he'd have to start a new tactic to make her realize exactly how deeply his feelings ran for her. How his days began with thoughts of her and how his heart ached for her when they were apart, filling when they were together—

She needed to know the depth of his emotions for her.

Was it too much to want? Too much to settle between them?

"Show me," Tallulah murmured as she moved into his arms. "Oh, Wyatt. Show me what you want."

He held her tightly, fearing he would awake from the dream and she would be gone. He buried his face into the sweet cove of her shoulder and throat and inhaled deeply. Her exotic feminine scent swirled around him. He was home, at least for a time. "Have you come to vamp me?" he asked unevenly against her skin.

"I'm sorry I didn't tell you about the baby in a different way," she whispered. "I'm sorry I didn't come with you when you asked. I hurt you, didn't I?"

"You're here now." Wyatt stroked the length of her back and prayed that Tallulah wouldn't leave him.

She smoothed the hair at the nape of his neck and the tense muscles of his shoulders. "Everything is just too new and too much," she whispered, shivering again.

Wyatt closed his eyes and cherished her warmth against him. Tallulah rested against him, her eyelashes fluttering against his throat. She held him tight as a small tremor ran through her. "Wyatt, there might not be a baby. I haven't seen a doctor. But the home pregnancy test says it's true."

"We'll see." Wyatt kissed her cheek and rocked her, praying that she cared for him. "If it's meant to be, we'll know soon enough. The first thing is to get you to a doctor. You just remember that I love you. I'm set in my ways, Tallulah Jane. I'm not likely to change."

"I'm new to this," Tallulah said shakily. She glanced around the compact interior and stared at the rumpled bed. "I've never tracked a man down before and cornered him in a tiny camper."

"Shy?" Wyatt loved her all the more for saving this experience for him.

Tallulah looked up at him and smoothed his hair gently. "What about you?"

"Can't say that I've ever been vamped in a camper before.... I think that is some getup," he murmured, looking down at the way her breasts pushed up plumply against his chest. If he wasn't mistaken, Tallulah was wearing a black lace bra.

His body tensed and heated with that thought. "This dress is nice. Pretty."

"'Nice.' Is that all? 'Nice'? Do you have any idea how much work it is for a woman to get into this garb?" she asked tightly. "Wyatt Remington, I want you to fully appreciate my scented bath and steaming my special dress that was in the closet for years. Dora Hines called and wanted me to sign up for one committee and Tex called and wanted me to come down and teach the new scorekeeper at the softball league. Then I had to wake up Norm to let him know I wouldn't be making pies...."

She frowned up at him as he continued to study her breasts and stroke her backside, gently cupping her against his rising passion. "I want you to know that 'keep my pig' isn't romantic, Wyatt. So I gave him to Dad to keep. Leroy was missing you and I would have brought him, but—"

Wyatt smoothed up the hem of the dress and eased his fingers into the lacy bands of her hose. "What's in the bag?"

"My nightie," Tallulah said as a blush began in her cheeks. She looked at his bare chest and traced patterns on it. "You'll have to step outside while I put it on. Ah...unless you'd rather I went to a hotel—"

Wyatt laughed with the joy rising in him; Tallulah frowned and shook her head.

"You are a strange man, Wyatt Remington," she stated thoughtfully.

Ten

When Wyatt ran his fingertips around the low-cut neckline of her dress, Tallulah tingled. "I don't know anything about you, Wyatt Sebastian."

He lifted an eyebrow. "Well, here's a tidbit. Sebastian was the name of some grand old great-grandfather, who established himself in the War Between the States. I have long suffered under the weight of wearing his name and prefer to wipe it from me."

His finger tugged lightly at her bodice, then slipped between her breasts. "You have wonderful breasts, my dear," he murmured. "A contrast in milky white and tips of dark rose. The reddish color entices me to a more Southern area of your anatomy, where the lush texture—"

"What an outrageous thing to say!" Tallulah shivered when Wyatt's strolling fingertip touched her nipples and they leaped to him, thrusting at the thin material. She flushed and realized that Wyatt's compliment had thrilled her, despite its intimacy. She leaned back, bracing her hips against the small table and gripped it, looking up at Wyatt's unshaven face as he reached across her to draw two candles from a shelf. "What are you doing?"

He slipped the candles into holders and flipped on a cassette player. Romantic violin music swirled around the small interior as he drew her into his arms. Tallulah resisted, eased back a bit and looked up at him. "I'm not certain that a man should talk to a woman about her body parts."

His hand reached down to cup her bottom and caress it leisurely. "My dear, you have never given me a chance to explore my seduction techniques. You have a go-for-it, hit-and-run style that leaves little breath for anything else but keeping up with you."

Tallulah smoothed the taut muscles of Wyatt's neck and shoulders. She placed her fingers on his chest and twirled them through the light layer of dark hair. "I would like to know why you haven't had a...an affair in years. From what I hear, that seems an abnormally long time for a man to abstain."

He brought her hand to his lips, kissing the fingertips. "I was saving my energies and my love for you, Tallulah Jane."

Tallulah inhaled as Wyatt kissed her cheek, then lower to play in the sensitive corners of her lips. "Mmm. Do you... do you think I am...do I satisfy you, Wyatt?"

"More than my dreams...." He kissed the other corner of her lips and Tallulah returned the tantalizing flick of his tongue.

"Wyatt? Do you...do you dream about me?" Tallulah was excited about the prospect. No man had ever said he'd dreamed about her. She held her breath. She had dreamed about Wyatt and if he did not to return the favor, she would crumble.

"I dream of you...at times I awake without you in my arms and I think I will expire," Wyatt whispered huskily as his hand inched down her zipper. He kissed her bare shoulder, nipping the skin slightly.

"Expire? Really?" Tallulah asked, not shielding the excitement racing through her as Wyatt drew down her dress. It slithered from her hips and she stepped free.

Wyatt stared down the length of her body, taking in her thigh-high hose. "My, my, Tallulah Jane. Aren't you a sight," he said in a rich appreciative tone.

"Wyatt...I am so frightened," she admitted shakily.

"Come here," he murmured gently, and pulled her against him. "I'm scared, too."

"You are?" She had not thought of Wyatt as a man wrapped in fear.

His smile moved against her cheek. "Sure. I fear losing you. Monogamous people don't roll along very well without their other half, you know.... Rather like a tire going *clumpety-clump, clumpety-clump* down an old lonesome road. I fear losing the joy you give me every day, just by looking at you.... I fear losing the warmth that grows inside me each time I see you."

He stroked her hair and nuzzled it. "You're my safety, Tallulah. My sunshine."

"Really?" Tallulah eased closer to him, excited about unwrapping this new Wyatt.

Wyatt's large hands released her bra; they skimmed away her briefs and he held her away from him.

"Then I have this fear that swallows me, makes me sweat and shiver every time I think of it."

"Oh, Wyatt. How awful. What is it?" she asked, concerned that something should so terrify Wyatt. She smoothed his cheeks, and the sound of razed stubble swept the still air.

"Well, why don't you get into bed, and I'll shave and tell you about it," he offered as he ran his hands under her bottom and lifted her against him. He nuzzled her breasts and kissed them gently, then he looked at her questioningly.

She wiggled her toes above the floor. "The camper is special made," Wyatt explained as he kissed her chin. "Had a foot added when they built it. Now, what about getting into bed while I shave?"

Moments later, Tallulah lay in Wyatt's narrow bed and watched him shave by candlelight. He hummed as he lathered with a bristly brush and used the old-fashioned straight razor. The scenario fascinated her. The leisurely process caused Wyatt's jaw to gleam when he finally patted away the bits of soapy foam.

"How interesting!" she exclaimed as he blew out the candles. "But, Wyatt, you never told me about your fear."

The sound of his jeans sliding to the floor stilled her. The sheet and light blanket lifted and cool air swept against her body. The small but comfortable bed sagged and Tallulah scooted back. Wyatt, lying beside her, took her hand and placed it over his heart. "Tallulah Jane, I have a deep terrifying fear that we will never make very slow, very complete love."

She swallowed and her heart raced. "I am sorry that you are unhappy, Wyatt," she began shakily.

"I'm not unhappy," he returned, turning on his side. "You're a generous woman, Tallulah. I feel very loved when at last you rest upon me. However, I await a slower mode of lovemaking. I'm not going anywhere. We could take our time."

"Making love slower?"

Wyatt eased away the sheets to kiss her throat, her shoulders, her breasts. He studied her and resisted her attempt to pull the sheet over her. "It's been on my mind that we might have a romantic evening—a movie or a dinner—and dance by candlelight. Then perhaps when the time was right, after a few slow kisses, we could retire. I don't want you to look back at our courtship and say, 'Old Wyatt needed lessons.'"

"Courtship?" she managed in a high, tight voice as he suckled at her breasts, treating them leisurely, and an intimate tugging began deep within her.

"You are a highly charged woman, Tallulah," Wyatt murmured as he kissed her navel and his hand cupped her femininity. His fingers slid within her so slowly that she held her breath. "I invite you to touch me, too," Wyatt offered huskily as he placed his cheek on her stomach, nestling against her.

Tallulah flexed her fingers against his shoulders, then traced the cords shifting beneath his skin. Wyatt kissed her stomach gently and her hips arched from the bed. "Wyatt—"

"Mmm?" He kissed an inch or two lower, then yielded to her tugging fingers in his hair. He eased over her. "Take me where you want me to be," he urged, after a long sweet kiss. "Warm me with your fire, for I have been a cold and lonely man without you."

Tallulah closed her eyes, reveling in Wyatt's rumbling tones, his old-fashioned, romantic use of words that swirled through her and heated her from head to toe. He continued to murmur his delight against her ear, shocking her until she caught his challenge—

She moved him very slowly, shyly, into her warmth, and Wyatt closed his eyes, his body trembling just once as he pushed deeper. He ran his hands beneath her hips and lifted her higher. Lodged firmly within her, filling her until she feared she might take him too soon, Wyatt whispered, "Now let's talk about what's between us. . . ."

"Talk?" Tallulah wrapped her legs around his hips and dug her fingertips into his arms, which were straining beside her. She squirmed; her body thrust against him and Wyatt eased back gently, only to fill her once more. "Talk? Wyatt, do something!"

"We are doing something, Tallulah," he reminded her in a tone laced with humor.

Now was not the time for Wyatt to become a funny man. She locked her arms around his neck and drew him down to her. "You stay put, Wyatt Remington."

"Can I tell you what I want? How much I desire you and how proud I am that you have come to me?" he asked slowly.

"Yes," she replied demurely, shocked at her need to hear him speak to her intimately.

As Wyatt spoke, he rubbed his chest against her breasts slowly, luxuriously. He tantalized the sensitive corners of her mouth until she reached up to lock his mouth against hers. Then the kiss changed. Wyatt was coming for her, taking her away from her fears.... He moved slightly away, looking fierce and strong above her, then returned to kiss her throat, finding the very pulse of her and placing his open mouth upon the beat. She caught him, nipped at his throat and gave herself to the fire between them.

"You are hot, Tallulah, a fire woman," he murmured roughly as she bit his shoulder to stop the pleasure—to keep him with her. "Very combustible."

Her hand slid between them and circled him and Wyatt stilled. She shivered, wondering if she had violated the male rules of lovemaking, and eased her hand away.

"You're going to pay for that, dear heart," Wyatt stated shakily.

"I shouldn't have—" She gasped as Wyatt's open mouth found her breasts. His hand swept between them and touched her in a certain place and she flamed, tightening and arching up against him.

"Exactly what do you think you are doing, Wyatt?" she demanded breathlessly when he allowed her to melt gently into the bed.

"I think I am loving you in a spiritual and physical mode, my heart," Wyatt rumbled unevenly, his hands trembling as he smoothed her hips. He moved slowly within her and she knew that Wyatt had further plans for her. "Please don't tell me otherwise . . . and *please* don't touch me now as you did a moment ago."

"I'm so sorry, Wyatt—"

"That is not the reason, dear heart," Wyatt stated between his teeth. "If you were to touch me now, the consequences would be dire."

She could not resist, and then Wyatt was giving his strength to her, and she was taking more, meeting him with all her strength, unafraid to touch him, to take him deeply into her heart and her body.

Wyatt braced away, breathing rapidly, his heart thudding heavily against hers. She looked at him and knew that he was waiting for her, waiting for her to love him. Tallulah pushed him down onto the bed and moved over him. She heard the rain slashing the roof, Wyatt's uneven breath and the creaking of the bed. When he held her breasts and cherished her, Tallulah closed her eyes, keeping the highest, most delicate throbbing within her.

He touched her again in that dark, private place and she ignited, taking him with her. There in the small nook of his camper, she reveled in the weight of Wyatt as he positioned himself over her strongly once more, while outside the storm waited and eased.

"I love you, Tallulah. Always will," he murmured unevenly as he began to move deeply within her, and for the second time, she clasped him close and pitted herself against his passion.

Several heartbeats later, she summoned enough strength to lift her head from Wyatt's chest. He had not left her, but was keeping her close to him. His expression was tender as they continued to study each other. "I want you to touch me as you want, dear heart," he said gently, smoothing her back and then her backside. "But there are times and there are times. Timing is everything. I had thought we would enjoy a slower pace."

Tallulah smiled sleepily. Wyatt was everything she wanted, tender, demanding, and her love of him filled her as she snuggled down to sleep. Wyatt eased her hand higher on his stomach and gathered her closer. "Wyatt? Are you certain that you are all right?" she asked, reminded of her desperate urge to gather him closer, too—how she had nipped his shoulder and—

Tallulah sat upright and pulled the sheet to her chest.

"Now what's wrong?" Wyatt asked.

"Are you certain that . . . that what we're doing is normal, Wyatt?"

"Normal as sweet-potato pie. I do believe we are about to embark upon a voyage of testing and enjoying and loving. I shiver when I think of the things awaiting us," he answered, drawing her back down to him. "It's because we have deep feelings for each other. The fire only draws us nearer, makes us like one."

"You say strange things, Wyatt. Strange things." Tallulah snuggled close to Wyatt's hard side and pressed her breasts against him. The aching eased a bit, and when Wyatt reached down to draw her thigh between his, she resisted.

"Come along now, Tallulah. Rest against me, with me," he ordered sleepily, then yawned.

"Can we sleep like this?" she asked as Wyatt fitted his hand over her breast.

"Sure can. Sweetest sleep in the whole world," he murmured. "Kiss me good-night now."

Tallulah awoke to Wyatt making love to her, his kisses tempting her to play awhile. She arched sleepily, stretching beneath him, and pushed her breasts against his pleasuring mouth.

Then the passion erupted again, and she gathered him close, fearing that he would move away, fearing that she had dreamed his hunger for her.

Wyatt's hushed shout quivered through her and she recognized the sound of her high, tight, muffled scream. He lay over her, his toes playing with hers as they kissed leisurely. Inspired to learn more delights, Tallulah kissed the corners of Wyatt's lips and he groaned reluctantly. "I have to go. It's my duty to open the tournament. You are to sleep here, in my bed, dreaming of me, Tallulah, dear heart. Then you are to find me...."

He kissed her very slowly, very thoroughly. "For I have plans for you."

"I can't stay here. Everyone will know," Tallulah whispered as Wyatt moved from the bed. The dim light slid across his backside and she looked away, only to return to the sight of his long, hard body.

He turned to gaze at her, a tall, hard male outlined by the dim light. She flushed, aware that Wyatt's need for her had not dimmed.

"You will have to decide what *you* want," Wyatt stated very carefully.

"Maybe I will stay," she returned slowly, admitting her need for him and what ran so strongly between them. Would their baby look like Wyatt? Was there a baby? She feared to see a doctor, to learn that the new life was not coming.

"How do you know I'm pregnant?" she asked baldly as Wyatt slipped into the tiny bathroom. The sound of water buried his reply, and she eased from the bed and stood. Her muscles were pleasantly strained, and she felt glorious—full of energy, full of loving....

"How do you know I'm pregnant, Wyatt?" she repeated as she opened the tiny shower door, to find Wyatt leaning his forehead against the side. He looked pale and shaky, and one hand was rubbing his stomach. "Are you all right? Ohmigosh, I've zapped you...strained you to an inch of your life! Oh, Wyatt, I am so sorry—"

He swallowed slowly and turned his best wet-orphan-pup look at her. "Oh, we are pregnant, all right," he said unevenly before gently shoving her out the door and closing it.

Tallulah found him at eleven o'clock. She felt energized, ready to face her old fears and dump them in the garbage.

Wyatt was the honored guest at the luncheon table, and when he saw her enter the hall, he rose and went to her. She admired the fit of his dark T-shirt and his faded denims; he eyed her body, which was clad in his denim shirt and his jeans, rolled up at the cuff. He noted her red-tinted toes within her newly purchased sandals and looked as though he'd like to suck them.

"Morning, dear heart," he murmured, and kissed her gently.

She pushed him back and glanced at the audience members, who were grinning like one big Cheshire cat. "You can't just do that in public, Wyatt."

"Sure I can. I want everyone to know you're my best girl."

The statement was youthful, silly and made her adore him more. She patted his hand when he glanced down at his quivering gelatin dessert and groaned.

At the afternoon fishing derby, Tallulah and Wyatt shared a boat on the fish-stocked lake. She learned that a man could sleep sitting upright and awaken instantly when a fish took his lure. She learned that he could lick fried chicken from her fingers while casting, and that when he was a little boy he'd terrorized his sisters with worms and grubs and fish guts. She learned that Wyatt was a gentleman about pit stops and unhooking her fish because she really didn't want to touch their slimy, wiggly bodies. Wyatt grinned wickedly when she said she was saving herself for her big one.

They returned to the camper to change for the casual dinner and Tallulah held her breath as Wyatt opened the

shopping sack to peer inside. "What's this?" he asked unevenly.

"Not much. Just a shirt and a pair of slacks. I had time
to shop a bit this morning. I hope they fit." She held her
clasped hands to her chest and wondered how many other
women had wanted to toss Wyatt on the camper's small bed
and vamp him.

"Thank you," he said in a humble tone as he studied the
pin-striped light blue shirt and the navy slacks. "Thank you
very much."

He was watching her so intently that Tallulah shivered.
"Your black boots won't match," she said, remembering
Jack's fastidious dislike for unmatched clothing. "I thought
the blue colors would set off your tan and dark hair and you
always wear black and—"

"I wear black because it's easy to match and I haven't had
a woman to fuss over me and keep me on my toes about
fashion."

"You could do with some new clothes, Wyatt," she said
defensively. "Fishing-line patches don't do a thing for you."

"So you care about me."

Triumph lurked in his tone and she eyed him warily,
stepping back a foot against the tiny table.

"You want to keep me warm in the winter, patch my
clothing, see that I am fed and happy, and you want to bear
my young. You want to create a home for us and become my
woman."

"You're reading an awful lot into this, Wyatt," she said
unevenly.

Wyatt tossed the sack onto the table and pulled her close.
Her breath went out of her as she recognized he was already aroused.

"I am taking heart. It occurs to me that if you wore my
clothes today. . . and you had time to shop. . . then perhaps
you wanted me near you all day. The thought encourages

and entices. If you bought me clothes, you'll have to dress me," he stated arrogantly.

"Not a chance—" she began as Wyatt's open, heated mouth found her breast. She locked his head to her fiercely and cried out with the beauty of his touch.

Then Wyatt rocked her against him. "You will actually have to touch my fly," he asserted.

"I am not afraid," she answered more boldly than she felt as Wyatt started to kiss her again.

She kissed him back; the impact of her body against his took him against the closet. Wyatt grasped the back of her neck with firm, gentle fingers and he held her still as he looked down at her. "Did you ever buy clothes for the backup boys?" he demanded, as if her answer was more crucial to him than air.

Tallulah shook her head. "Ball caps," she whispered.

"Good enough," he said in a tight, pleased tone. "I don't want to hear about your ex-husband," he added grimly.

Tallulah gripped his T-shirt in her hands and thrust her face up to his. "Well, you're going to. I never bought Jack's clothes. He didn't trust me to coordinate. There...I've never told anyone that."

His eyes lit beneath his shielding lashes, scorching her with his heat. Then Wyatt's mouth took hers hungrily, possessively, sparing her no escape.... Tallulah gave back her passion without mercy.

She had him there against the wall and Wyatt held her close when they were finished. Tallulah mulled over their passionate lovemaking and wondered if they were abnormal. She wondered if women attacked men, ravaged them and cried out so loudly. She already knew some men weren't as responsive and didn't appreciate her athletic strength as Wyatt apparently did. He seemed to revel in her clasping him close and in her eagerness to become one with him.

"I'd carry you to the bed," he offered huskily, "but my jeans are around my ankles."

She tested his jeans that she had worn that day and found that she had to step out of them. She braced her hands against him, noting that the camper slanted oddly. "What was that big whump?"

Wyatt rubbed his chest against her breasts, a movement he enjoyed and did frequently. "Love hitting us sideways, at a time when we least expected it. Either that or the trailer hitch hitting the ground."

"Why is the camper slanting?" she asked, testing her balance and moving away slightly. Wyatt was looking at her in that quiet dark way he did when he mentioned love.

"Because I think you love me, Tallulah. And because you touched my fly and the world didn't end. And because tonight after the ceremonies, we're moving this camper into a place very private."

When Wyatt pulled into Elegance's city limits, it was high noon the next day. He looked in the rearview mirror of his pickup. Tallulah's canary yellow pickup was still following him. He forced his fingers to uncurl from the steering wheel and realized his palms were damp.

He glanced at Tallulah's driveway, inhaled and gripped the steering wheel again. Then he drove by her house, eyeing her truck in the side-view mirror. The vehicle slowed at her driveway, then continued following him.

He waved to Fallon, who was pulling a red wagon loaded with Miracle and filled grocery sacks. Her face lit and she grinned, giving him a thumbs-up, go-for-it sign, then pointed to the canary yellow truck close behind him. Fallon would not likely be as happy with a suggestion Wyatt intended to make—he wanted Fallon to notify her mother of her location. Michelle, as twisted as she had been, might have changed, and Wyatt knew a parent's pain of losing a child. And Tallulah's suggestion of an educational plan for Fallon would have his support. His daughter had missed so much of what she deserved and Wyatt wanted everything the future could offer her.

He inhaled the mountain air and sunshine and counted his blessings so far. His daughter's smile was wide and open; Tallulah was wearing a puzzled scowl.

He wiped the cold sweat from his upper lip and realized that he hadn't taken time to shave this morning. He'd been too distracted by Tallulah's long legs beneath his borrowed T-shirt as she'd moved around the campfire, cooking breakfast. Sharing the same bucket of heated water had become an interesting affair of soap bubbles and washcloths and laughter.

His body tensed as he passed the Tall Order and the little pickup slowed again, only to continue following him. He waved to Norm and a cluster of Elegance residents, who stood on the sidewalk and watched him pass.

They were also seeing Tallulah pass. He noted her wave to her father and a prim straightening of her glasses, as if she would not be questioned about her destiny.

Wyatt clamped his fingers on the steering wheel. *Her destiny was with one Wyatt Remington.*

He was pushing now, his stomach tight with the fear that Tallulah would choose not to come after him. Wyatt pulled his pickup and camper into the driveway of another house, a house that he had just purchased, a home where Tallulah had not lived with her ex-husband. He glanced in the mirror and saw the yellow pickup pull into the driveway behind him.

"This is that architect's place—Woodrow Scats. He built this thing, then decided he didn't like rural life and Elegance's social life—bingo parties and softball," Tallulah noted when they were standing side by side on the front sidewalk.

Wyatt inhaled her fresh scent, grateful that she did not smell of onions at this one moment. He glanced down the long, lean length of her dressed in his clothing and realized how very proud he was of her....

Tallulah took in the jutting ultra-modern wooden affair that rambled over the small knoll above Elegance. Surrounded by pines, firs and quaking aspens that would soon turn into their fall oranges and yellows, the house looked sterile and gloomy. A rubble of rocks, boards, and bulldozer dirt served as the front landscape.

Wyatt placed his hand on Tallulah's shoulder and waved to Jess Hawkins and a small group of curious residents. He closed his eyes when her arm slid around his waist and stayed, her fingers hooked lightly in his belt. "Well, here goes," he said, taking his fears in hand and scooping Tallulah off her feet.

He carried her up the front walkway and up the stairs.

When the door closed behind them and they were surrounded by barren wood walls and faced with the enormous rock fireplace, Wyatt slowly placed Tallulah on her feet.

She brushed silky red-gold hair away from her hot cheek and pushed her palms against his chest. "The whole town saw that— Emily Jackson is the worst gossip and she'll catch the people who missed you acting like— Do you know what that looked like, Wyatt Remington? Do you know? I'll tell you what it looked like . . . like we've just had a romantic rendezvous and you've brought me home to be your bride—"

Tallulah stopped, placed her hand over her mouth and eyed him from behind her huge lenses.

Wyatt removed her glasses. "That's about the true size of it," he agreed gently. "Winter is coming, dear heart. We can't keep knocking the camper off its hitch, and I sure as hell will not live with you in a home you shared with another man. There's a room upstairs that would make a perfect nursery. Several rooms for more kids, if you want. And there's a big one downstairs that will be perfect for your father when he gets a bit older. If Fallon wants to live here and you're for it, we can modify to give her privacy."

She placed her hands on her hips and eyed him warily. "You're not making this easy, Wyatt."

"Never said I would," he returned with a firmness that did not ring true to himself. Wyatt slid his shaking hands inside his back pockets and braced himself against losing the woman who was his wife—at least in his heart.

"Uh-huh." Tallulah looked up at him evenly and jammed her glasses back on her nose. "Well . . . I'll just be going now," she said lightly.

Then she walked out the door.

Eleven

_____

Wyatt listened to the lonely sound of the wind sliding off the mountains and swirling around his new house. It was just a shell, needing Tallulah to make it a home.

Within two weeks, September would sweep across the mountains and the snow would begin falling in the high country. When he had signed the contract to buy the house, he'd had visions of cuddling her by the fire...visions of revealing what was dear to him, the things he'd never shared with another person....

He glanced around his new Tallulahless house. At eleven o'clock in the evening of the same day that had started with her snuggling close, he was certain to notice that she was missing—replaced by the shadows that had been with him for a lifetime. He grimaced at Leroy, who was snoozing in front of the small fire in the grate. The red bandannas tied around his neck stated that the porker had been pampered by a horde of women and had changed loyalties.

Wyatt braced one boot on the fireplace grate and studied the fire, trying to read the answers in the flames. The house loomed around him, angular, shadowy and cold. Wyatt rubbed his bare chest and wondered what he knew about making a home. What did he know about living in one place, signing up for leagues and committees and living day-to-day with one person?

The tense muscles of his jaw ached and Wyatt ran his hand across his face, realizing that his beard would be thick and black now. "Gothic guy," he muttered grimly as he gazed in the huge window-to-floor mirror.

With shadows clinging to his face, hollowing his eyes, and his beard catching the firelight, he looked as though he could loom out of a Stephen King thriller.

The lights of Elegance spread out before him, twinkling in the homes of families who loved one another. Tallulah's yard light dimmed and Wyatt closed his eyes, wishing for her, willing her to want him.

The camper mattress lay in a corner near the fireplace, reminding him of Tallulah's warmth.

He forced himself to uncurl his fingers. He wanted a life with her enough to wait and try again— The next time he got Tallulah close, he wouldn't make any mistakes about reeling her in—

Wyatt closed his eyes. He had pushed too hard and she had run from ties with him.

There was one tie that she could not deny; Wyatt realized suddenly that the stirring within him as they'd made love that first time had reason. In his deepest primitive senses, sheltered from reality, he had known that he was giving her his child.

A baby. If Wyatt was certain of anything, he was certain of their baby nestling in Tallulah's warmth.

He swallowed unevenly and realized that he had been holding his breath. A generous, caring woman, Tallulah by nature was sharing and she would not withhold his child from him.

Feeling worn and tired, Wyatt ran his hands over his face, then braced them against the wall. He pushed against the paneling, wanting to shove the shadows away and to have Tallulah near—

Tallulah had come to him once; why did he have to push his luck? Who did he think he was, setting rules for a relationship between them? Why did he have to tell her that he loved her, when Tallulah clearly had been scarred by love?

Wyatt eased into a folding lawn chair, crossed his hands on his stomach and, in the firelight, mulled over his mistakes. He picked up the newly installed telephone on the varnished boards beside him, began to dial Tallulah's number, then replaced the receiver on the cradle.

The empty house tore at him—the immense master bedroom overlooking Elegance, the nursery, the kitchen that could be filled with life and loving, sat empty.

The woman he loved had run from him.

"Good Lord, Wyatt. You're enough to scare any woman," he muttered darkly. Leroy grunted a sleepy agreement. Wyatt shook his head. After two nights of Tallulah's loving, he'd had other plans for this night. He dragged a shirt she had worn from his suitcase and draped it over his bare chest. After a moment, he eased the sleeves around his neck.

Wyatt inhaled her fragrance and stroked the denim over his chest; he drew one cuff to his lips, kissed it and then kissed the other, before arranging them back on his neck. He smoothed the cloth over his chest and wished for Tallulah's curves.

Leroy oinked in his sleep, his hooves moving as though he were running. "Huh. Not exactly the patter of the little feet I want," Wyatt muttered, reaching to draw the jeans that Tallulah had worn over his lap.

He wrapped the jean legs around his hips and sat there, watching the firelight and caressing the empty denim across his chest.

Very little kept him from going to her— He had to give her time to think, to decide what she wanted from him—

The telephone rang and Wyatt jerked the receiver to his ear. His fist closed about the denim shirt and he prayed that the call was from Tallulah.

There was a sob, someone blew their nose, and Tallulah stated huskily, "You've got a lot to learn, bozo."

"This isn't an 'I love you,' is it?" he asked tensely, his heartbeat ripping through him as he waited.

She ignored his question with one of hers. "My doilies won't match that modern house."

Wyatt breathed slowly, methodically, wading through his impatient emotions, before he said quietly, "We'll build another one."

"Houses aren't important, Wyatt. You know that."

"Yes.... I know what is important. I love you, Tallulah," he stated slowly, firmly.

There was a long silence, a sniff, then Tallulah said quietly, "I have to know that you want me because of me. Not because you feel that you have to."

Wyatt eased to his feet, cradling the telephone in one hand and keeping the denim shirt in his fist. "Where do you want us to spend the night?" he asked carefully. "Because that is where I want to tell you again how much I love you and want you."

"Get this— You don't have to marry me, Wyatt. I'll see you tomorrow," she said before the line silenced. Wyatt listened to the empty buzz for a long time before he went to stand in front of the huge windows.

He sensed that Tallulah needed the night, but not going to her was agony.

Tallulah jammed the second gear of her pickup, an unusual occurrence. On the seat beside her, the basket filled with wine, long-stemmed glasses and a romantic dinner shuddered. She placed a firm hand on the basket and shivered.

At eight o'clock in the evening, the streets of Elegance were empty. She had planned the exact hour, giving the residents enough time to settle in front of their television sets; she didn't want to be their spectator sport as she drove up to Wyatt's house without her headlamps on.

A red blinking light over a patrol car appeared in her rearview mirror and Tallulah eased her pickup to the side of the highway. Roy Marshall, clad in his uniform and packing his nightstick, Mace, handcuffs and big pistol, loomed by her open window.

Tallulah smiled tightly up at him. Not even a three-hundred-pound policeman would stop her from completing her mission to tell Wyatt she loved him. She greeted the lawman. "Roy."

"Tallulah. Nice night, huh?"

He peered down into her cab and noted the bottle of wine sticking out of the basket. He grinned, noting her hair, which was curled and perched on top of her head, her eye shadow and glossy lips and the low neckline of her new, tight red dress. She tapped her new red shoes-to-match on the floorboard while Roy took his time surmising her goal.

"What's this? Little Red Riding Hood on her way to see the wolf?" Roy asked with a chuckle.

His flashlight found her overnight bag on the passenger floorboard, then the beam roamed the bed of her truck. The vehicle was laden with her clothing, cleaning supplies, small antique furniture and a variety of boxes, all tightly strapped. His big hand rested on her softball bat and he grinned again, looking like a huge, toothy Cheshire cat.

"Come down to the café tomorrow, Roy. I'll bake you a special high-meringue pie," she offered.

"I'd prefer banana cream," he returned. "I guess you're headed up to that daffy architect's castle to see your old man. Did you remember the romantic cassette tapes?"

She had, but she scowled up at him and Roy chuckled anew. He patted the roof of her pickup cab and nodded toward the "daffy architect's castle." "Don't worry about my pie tomorrow, Stretch. I'll collect when you're back in the baking mode."

"What's that supposed to mean?" she demanded, almost straightening from her slump. It was a practiced slump to avoid crunching her hair on the roof; she had to protect her new puffy feminine hairdo with elaborate little wisps around her ears and her nape.

Roy shook his head. "You're a good-looking woman, Tallulah. And Wyatt's a good man. He makes the best double-decker cheeseburgers I've ever tasted.... Keep him here. By the way, when you see him, tell him that I've got a pretty little female pig that needs a boyfriend real soon."

"You are interfering with a romantic voyage here, Roy," she stated ominously. "My pilgrimage to my betrothed. A bridal journey to my beloved.... The potential father of my child and the mate of my heart— You just wait until some girl packs up her dowry and comes calling on you."

She aimed a meaningful look at him. "I'm a talented matchmaker, Roy. I could fix you up with a real witch."

For a moment Roy appeared poleaxed. Then he flushed, stammered and said, "Don't forget Venus, my girl porker, has a short attention span."

"You are an unromantic man, Roy Marshall," she stated archly as she eased the pickup into gear and continued on her way. She glared in the rearview mirror as Roy's siren gave one teasing whoop.

She pulled into the driveway, parking behind Wyatt's truck. It hadn't moved all day... or so said her father, who had established a Main Street stakeout party. One of the team, Elmer Jones, had noted Leroy trotting down Main

Street to Fallon's house. Another of the team followed at a safe distance to see the porker safely admitted to the house by a very happy little girl.

Tallulah surmised her emotions—they balled into one big I-am-scared.

She checked her body's reactions—she was cold and hot and queasy and trembling.

She surveyed her mental condition. It read now or never, go for it, what have you got to lose, and he doesn't stand a chance. She tossed away the faint-heart thought. Wyatt wasn't fair or a damsel; he was very male, big and ominous when he wanted...with Gothic pasted all over him.

Tallulah counted her pluses— Wyatt seemed to appreciate her athletic endeavors. He had designed his best lure and had given it her name. He'd said he loved her, and Wyatt Remington always told the truth.

She trusted him.

She *loved* and trusted him, she corrected.

After a sleepless night of wrestling with her pillows, almost running to Wyatt last night, she had stayed home all day. She'd rambled through the house, touching mementos that she once had cherished and that now meant nothing without Wyatt. Around noon, she began packing the essentials—cleaning supplies, blankets, her clothing and toiletries. She folded her great-grandmother's quilts, which told stories of the pioneers, and placed them into a box; her mother's cookbooks and Irish-linen tablecloths and napkins were packed into a special carton. She began packing several of her small, beloved antiques into the pickup bed.

At three o'clock, she hurried down to the dry-goods store and shopped for the perfect, man-slayer dress with matching red-hot undies. To emphasize her long legs, which Wyatt seemed to appreciate with delight, she chose thigh-high hose with black seams.

She shifted uneasily, sliding her fingers into the dress to adjust her slip's straps. She had eliminated the push-up bra at the last minute, since it oversensitized her already aching breasts.

Tallulah shook her head and noted that her curls bobbed when she did. She did it again. It took a good man to appreciate all her work. If Wyatt seemed taken with her outfit, she'd set about some in-depth, man-killing shopping time. His reaction to her basic short black dress had been ego lifting. She couldn't wait to model her new black-lace shorty nightgown with matching string panties—Wyatt had not allowed her time to show it off while they were—

While they were making love.

Now she knew that Wyatt was telling her with his body, was promising her tomorrows—

She knew what he'd wanted when he'd carried her over the threshold of his house.

Tallulah placed her hand over her rapidly beating heart and watched the dark house. She wanted to tell Wyatt in the most romantic way that she loved him.

That she knew that she had always loved him and that she wanted what the future would bring—with him.

She placed her palms over the tiny life that she was certain lay within her.

A family man, that's what Wyatt was.... Tallulah had seen his love for his sisters and his love for Fallon and Miracle.

A loving man, patient, gentle and giving.

Tallulah inhaled and braced herself. "Prepare yourself, Wyatt Sebastian Remington. For I have come to claim you," she murmured, then inhaled the brand-new, sexy perfume she had dabbed upon appropriate body places.

She checked the tiny lump tucked in her pocket. Romancing a man with wine and a candlelight dinner and telling him of her love needed an extra touch. The plain gold band was important to her. She wanted Wyatt wearing her gift every day, to remind him of her love.

Tallulah inhaled the cool evening air and thought about the coming winter.

Because she really had plans for that first winter with Wyatt. He was not escaping her. Since his camper steamed at the seams when they made love, they might have to raise the fire insurance on the wooden house.

She eased her hair out of the pickup and then her body. With her heels on, she could look at Wyatt eyeball-to-eyeball when she told him of her love. She walked around the pickup and carefully lifted the picnic basket free, then placed the shoulder strap of her overnight bag over her shoulder.

She began to walk up the walkway to the house, telling herself to be patient, to give Wyatt the romance he deserved. She'd take her time, and when the moment was right, she'd tell him of her love.

Tallulah closed her eyes, prayed that she would give Wyatt his due and knocked at the wooden door.

It swung open slightly, and fearing for him, she called, "Wyatt?"

Tallulah shivered, searching the shadowy interior of the barren room, the firelight glistening on the varnished floor and the paneled walls. What if Wyatt had fallen down the stairs? What if he had decided to leave after her call? "Wyatt?" she called again, fear racing through her.

"I'm here," he murmured at her side, taking away her bag and the basket and placing them on the floor.

When he straightened, Wyatt looked at her. His face looked as hard as when she had met him, the lines deeply grooved. The shadows beneath his eyes were new and haunting and she knew how he had suffered through the day and night. He was dressed in the clothing she had given him. His black beard gleamed in the firelight and she explored it with her fingertips, loving the crisp, warm texture. "I was cutting wood out back—working off a little tension—when

I saw your pickup. I didn't have time to shave," he stated unevenly.

"You're so beautiful," she said, meaning it as she drew his mouth down to hers. "Don't be nervous."

She tasted her dreams on his lips, found his hunger and the safety of his arms coming slowly, gently, around her.

She breathed the fresh soapy scents of his hair and ran her fingers through the damp texture. She pressed against him and fitted her body to his, two matching hearts beating rapidly against each other. His beard tickled against her cheek as they stood still, arms wrapped around each other. The closeness was enough for now, the realization that their moment was near, the commitments of the hearts to be renewed in the firelight and in the dawn and in the days and nights of the future together.

She stroked his back and realized how tense he was. She knew how much waiting for her had cost him....

"I am home, Wyatt Sebastian," she said in the grand, old-fashioned style that was his when he was deeply moved. "I am home."

Wyatt's hard body trembled against her. For an instant his arms tightened around her as though he feared losing her. Tallulah closed her eyes and reveled in her joy, then she stepped back and looked at him. "You are mine, Wyatt, and I want to give you a night you'll remember."

"Do tell," he invited, his gaze roaming slowly down her body, then lifting to note the curls high on top of her head. "You're a fine catch," he said huskily, appreciatively.

"I am a keeper, Wyatt," she corrected him gently, and licked her lips to invite his attention.

"A real nice keeper," he agreed, touching the glossy, soft texture with his fingertip.

"You're not too bad a catch yourself," she returned, placing her hand over his heart and leaning to kiss him.

Wyatt rolled over Tallulah, pinning her beneath him. He caught her wrists and held her hands away from him. "Say it again," he demanded, his expression fierce, the elemental male, stark and powerful in the firelight. His shaggy hair softened his jutting cheekbones, the dark shadows of his eyes.

Their bodies were locked as tightly as their hearts, which were beating together, straining to become perfect—

"I love you, Wyatt Remington.... I will love you with all my being for all time," she declared.

He closed his eyes and shuddered, releasing her wrists. She placed her fingers on his damp cheekbones, easing back the rumpled, thick wave from his brow. Her fingertip trailed across his lashes and came away moist. "It's true, isn't it?" he asked carefully, his gaze slowly leaving her face to move slowly down their bodies, gleaming in the firelight.

"True as the sky and the wind and the mountains.... I love you...."

"I love you, Tallulah," Wyatt murmured, bending to kiss the tears of joy flowing down her cheeks.

"Prove it," she challenged, even though she knew that when this time of their lives was a memory, the heated bonding of flesh, the love that ran deeply between them would keep them warm.

But Wyatt wasn't taking orders...at least not just yet. He framed her face with his hands, his thumbs stroking the line of her cheekbones and smoothing her temples. "If there is a baby—and I'm certain there is—he will only deepen what is already between us."

"I know...an enrichment of our love." Tallulah lifted to kiss him tenderly. She knew that Wyatt would share the happiness or the sadness in their lives; he'd be there in the dawn, the sunlight and the night. "I know," she whispered again, then kissed the ring that gleamed on his finger.

"I do so love you, Tallulah," Wyatt affirmed, and lowered his mouth to find the sensitive corners of her lips.

She gasped, arched and shivered against him. "How do you know I love that?"

"I'm a sportsman, a champion angler," he murmured, moving to the other side of her mouth. "Our instincts are unerring. They have to be. Keepers aren't that easy to catch, you know. They're quirky and wary and—"

"Mr. Easy," Tallulah teased with a loving smile. Then she set about demonstrating her new skills as a worthy challenger to his abilities, and Wyatt stopped talking.

Epilogue

"**D**addy, the posse is coming," four-year-old Cherish squealed, scrambling up on the bed. Wyatt opened one eye and glanced at the dawn spreading out beyond the master bedroom's window.

He stretched, yawned and wrapped himself in the warmth of his life. He savored the scents and the busy sounds around him, the household stirring at dawn. Each day was better than the one before, more exciting, more rich with texture and love.

His lonely, dark, hard road lay behind him and sunlight lay ahead— Cherish bounced on him gently, reminding Wyatt of her presence.

He'd wept when she was born, unable to shield his joy. Tallulah had taken his hand to her mouth, kissing his palm, and though her eyes had been shadowed with the child-birth, they had told him of her love.

"Daddy?" Cherish prompted impatiently, bouncing on his back. "Are you awake?"

"Is it the dreaded pink posse?" he asked, faking a fearful tone. On the first day of fishing season, the pink posse would be out to get him. They needed him to unhook their fish and clean them.

The pink posse couldn't stand fish guts. They "oooh-ed" and "yuk-ed" and looked at him with pleading eyes. The older pink posse, his sisters, had never liked that particular phase of fishing, either.

A tousled tomboy at four years old, Cherish wiggled down beside him, then pulled the sheet over his head. "I'll hide you, Daddy," his miniature version of Tallulah stated protectively as she climbed up on him. She perched innocently on his back, awaiting the posse. "Mommy must not like her nightgown. She keeps taking it off," Cherish noted, lifting the sheet to peer down at him. "She's wearing your pajama top, but she left you the bottoms. You should get her a nightie like mine, long and soft with pink pigs on it."

From the bottom of the stairs, Leroy squealed his agreement, racing through the house with the posse.

"That's a good idea," Wyatt agreed as Cherish's moist kiss met his. She dusted a rose petal from his beard and plucked another from his shoulder, studying it and frowning. "Daddy, do you know there are flowers all over Mommy's and your bed?"

"The flower fairies came in the night." Tallulah made an excellent five-foot-eleven-inch flower fairy.

Cherish covered his head with the sheet again and Wyatt closed his eyes, remembering how Tallulah had modeled her new negligee.

Beneath the sheet, Wyatt awaited the posse and counted his blessings. Cherish's bottom squirmed over his back as she impatiently awaited the other females. "Don't you worry, Daddy," she whispered in a conspiratorial tone. "I'll hide you, then you can help me catch the big one.... 'Cause I'm your special little keeper," she stated firmly, using his endearment for her.

Wyatt caught his wife's scent in the pillows and spanned his hand over the warmth she had just vacated. Through the adjustment of sharing their lives and children, through the dark days and the joy, their love increased with each heartbeat.

Their family was expanding.... There was Fallon, who had changed into a vibrant, strong woman. She was taking college classes now and Miracle was a busy first grader. Fallon had come to terms with her past and sadly recognized the damage her mother had done. His daughter grew closer to him each day and had recently changed her name to Remington.

There was Heather, abandoned at six and just beginning to love her adopted family...and Joey, a five-year-old, discarded by her mother because she could not hear...and Mary Lynn, who had lived in foster homes until they adopted her at ten years old.... The Wyatt Remingtons of Elegance had recently adopted two more girls, Sylvia and Vanessa, busy eight-year-olds.

Cherish's round bottom squirmed again, and Wyatt patted it. Tallulah had moved through pregnancy with an impatience that was typical, nurturing Wyatt when he was at his weakest. She was at her height commanding and tending the pink posse, and loving every minute.

Wyatt inhaled her scent, wallowing in his full, happy life. He especially loved the moments when they escaped into the privacy of the camper and a secluded pine nook. Tallulah's father or Fallon took charge of the crew then and when Tallulah traveled with him on short trips. The new all-girl Remington softball team was already carving a fine athletic reputation. The backup boys, who helped, had their hands full with the energetic little girls.

The W. R. Lures Catalog had a whole raft of beautiful new lures named for each child, especially designed by Wyatt.

He recognized the scent of the woman he loved, his wife, his heart, Tallulah. Her weight settled on the bed beside him and he reached to mold her robe-covered backside. Her fingers caught and linked with his, just as their lives were woven together.

"I want a kiss," he whispered dramatically.

"Shh. We're hiding you. The pink posse is roaming through the house. Leroy is acting as scout."

"Grr," he said, making hungry, growling noises, which he knew delighted Tallulah—especially when he made them against her throat.

"Are you guys going to start that kissing stuff again?" Cherish asked impatiently as Tallulah eased under the sheet and Wyatt gathered her close.

"Love you," he murmured, rubbing her nose with his.

"Love you back," she returned tenderly, laying her hand on his unshaven cheek and kissing him. "No more shadows."

"Nothing but good times and sunshine," he had time to say, before the pink posse swarmed into their bedroom and piled into the bed, giggling wildly.

Wyatt surrendered, lying back against the pillows and the rose petals; he did his best to return a portion of the girls' impatient, hurried kisses all over his face. Then he grinned at Tallulah and winked. "You know what? I feel like going fishing today. Let's all pack up and go fishing."

"You are Mr. Easy," she said lovingly, taking the hand he had lifted to her.

*   *   *   *   *

SILHOUETTE

SPECIAL EDITION

The Family Way

Popular author **Gina Ferris Wilkins** has written a warm and wonderful new mini-series for us at Silhouette Special Edition, which we are sure you're going to love.

A fond grandmother wants to see all her grandchildren happily married but, of course, it isn't quite that simple!

Enjoy the emotion in:

October 1995
A MAN FOR MUM

December 1995
A MATCH FOR CELIA

February 1996
A HOME FOR ADAM

June 1996
CODY'S FIANCÉE

COMING NEXT MONTH

MYSTERIOUS MOUNTAIN MAN
Annette Broadrick

Man of the Month

Rebecca Adams needed Jake Taggart. Only he could save her company. But he was living halfway up a mountain and she was going to have to go and get him. They'd be alone in the wilderness…

IMPULSE
Lass Small

Amy Allen took one look at Chas Cougar and decided she just had to meet him, so she decided to pose as a distant cousin and gate-crash the wedding he was attending. Chas knew right away Amy wasn't kin, but he could change that…if she was willing to be wed!

THE COP AND THE CHORUS GIRL
Nancy Martin

Opposites Attract

A cop couldn't ignore a female in distress, but it was unusual for a bride to rush away from the church before the wedding, which was why Patrick Flynn didn't react as quickly as Dixie wanted. Now he was going to have to fight off her gangster groom.

▼ SILHOUETTE

Desire

COMING NEXT MONTH

DREAM WEDDING
Pamela Macaluso

Just Married

Once Alex would have sold his soul to kiss Genie. Now his "dream girl" was a prim teacher and the swot she'd rejected, who'd turned into a strapping, sexy CEO, was back for revenge.

HEAVEN CAN'T WAIT
Linda Turner

Spellbound

Prudence Sullivan knew Zeb Murdock was the lover for whom she'd waited centuries. Unfortunately, although he felt the fire between them, Murdock was determined to resist her. Pru couldn't allow that!

FORSAKEN FATHER
Kelly Jamison

Rachel Tucker had to resist rekindling the past—or risk revealing the secret she should have told John McClennon years ago. She had to protect her son.

COMING NEXT MONTH FROM

 **SILHOUETTE**

Sensation

A thrilling mix of passion, adventure and drama

RESTLESS WIND Nikki Benjamin
POINT OF NO RETURN Rachel Lee
NIGHTSHADE Nora Roberts
STILL MARRIED Diana Whitney

Intrigue

Danger, deception and desire— new from Silhouette...

UNDER THE KNIFE Tess Gerritsen
RISKY BUSINESS M.J. Rodgers
GUILTY AS SIN Cathy Gillen Thacker
PRIVATE EYES Madeline St. Claire

Special Edition

Satisfying romances packed with emotion

A MAN FOR MUM Gina Ferris Wilkins
A SECRET AND A BRIDAL PLEDGE Andrea Edwards
DOES ANYONE KNOW WHO ALLISON IS?
Tracy Sinclair
TRULY MARRIED Phyllis Halldorson
A STRANGER IN THE FAMILY Patricia McLinn
A PERFECT SURPRISE Caroline Peak

A years supply of Silhouette Desires – absolutely free!

Would you like to win a years supply of seductive and breathtaking romances? Well, you can and they're FREE! All you have to do is complete the wordsearch puzzle below and send it to us by 31st March 1996. The first 5 correct entries picked after that date will win a years supply of Silhouette Desire novels (six books every month — worth over £150). What could be easier?

STOCKHOLM	PARIS	HELSINKI	ANKARA
REYKJAVIK	LONDON	ROME	AMSTERDAM
COPENHAGEN	PRAGUE	VIENNA	OSLO
MADRID	ATHENS	LIMA	

N	O	L	S	O	P	A	R	I	S
E	Q	U	V	A	F	R	O	K	T
G	C	L	I	M	A	A	M	N	O
A	T	H	E	N	S	K	E	I	C
H	L	O	N	D	O	N	H	S	K
N	S	H	N	R	I	A	O	L	H
E	D	M	A	D	R	I	D	E	O
P	R	A	G	U	E	U	Y	H	L
O	A	M	S	T	E	R	D	A	M
C	R	E	Y	K	J	A	V	I	K

Please turn over for details on how to enter ➤

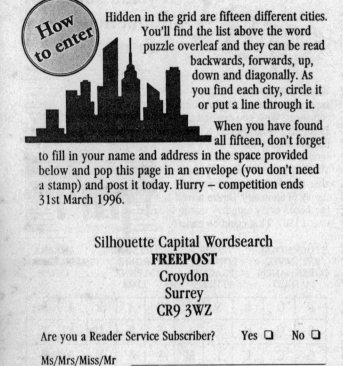

How to enter

Hidden in the grid are fifteen different cities. You'll find the list above the word puzzle overleaf and they can be read backwards, forwards, up, down and diagonally. As you find each city, circle it or put a line through it.

When you have found all fifteen, don't forget to fill in your name and address in the space provided below and pop this page in an envelope (you don't need a stamp) and post it today. Hurry – competition ends 31st March 1996.

Silhouette Capital Wordsearch
FREEPOST
Croydon
Surrey
CR9 3WZ

Are you a Reader Service Subscriber?   Yes ❑   No ❑

Ms/Mrs/Miss/Mr   _____

Address _____

_____

_____ Postcode _____

One application per household.

You may be mailed with other offers from other reputable companies as a result of this application. If you would prefer not to receive such offers, please tick box.   ❑   COMP295
                                                                          C